"RAND, DON'T LOOK AT ME," KAT WHISPERED. "I don't want you to look at me. I look like hell from all this crying."

"I don't want to look at you," he said. "I only want to kiss you. I have my eyes closed." There was a hint of laughter in his voice, and she let him tilt her face up. She risked a peek between swollen lids. He did have his eyes, shut. his thick black lashes fluttering slightly on his cheeks.

Even with his eyes closed, he found her mouth with unerring accuracy, and she felt a shiver course through her. It was answered by the one that shook him as he wrapped his arms around her and drew her firmly into his embrace.

It began as a gentle kiss, but his need was so great, his mouth was suddenly hard and seeking, hot and demanding.

Kat's head swam as they kissed, yearning for something lost . . . and maybe found again. Had anyone ever kissed her like Rand did? He put everything he had, everything he was, into his kisses. Deep, rich, voluptuous, they could turn a woman inside out in only a moment . . . .

WHAT ARE *LOVESWEPT* ROMANCES?

They are stories of true romance and touching emotion. We believe those two very important ingredients are constants in our highly sensual and very believable stories in the LOVESWEPT *line. Our goal is to give you, the reader, stories of consistently high quality that may sometimes make you laugh, sometimes make you cry, but are always fresh and creative and contain many delightful surprises within their pages.*

Most romance fans read an enormous number of books. Those they truly love, they keep. Others may be traded with friends and soon forgotten. We hope that each LOVESWEPT *romance will be a treasure—a "keeper." We will always try to publish*

LOVE STORIES YOU'LL NEVER FORGET
BY AUTHORS YOU'LL ALWAYS REMEMBER

The Editors

Loveswept ® 678

KISS AND MAKE UP

JUDY
GILL

BANTAM BOOKS
NEW YORK · TORONTO · LONDON · SYDNEY · AUCKLAND

KISS AND MAKE UP

A Bantam Book / April 1994

*If you would be interested in receiving protective vinyl covers for your
Loveswept books, please write to this address for information:*

Loveswept
Bantam Books
P.O. Box 985
Hicksville, NY 11802

ISBN 0-553-44263-5

Published simultaneously in the United States and Canada

*Bantam Books are published by Bantam Books, a division of Bantam Dou-
bleday Dell Publishing Group, Inc. Its trademark, consisting of the words
"Bantam Books" and the portrayal of a rooster, is Registered in U.S. Patent
and Trademark Office and in other countries. Marca Registrada. Bantam
Books, 1540 Broadway, New York, New York 10036.*

PRINTED IN THE UNITED STATES OF AMERICA

OPM   0 9 8 7 6 5 4 3 2 1

KISS AND
MAKE UP

ONE

Kat squinted against the spraying disinfectant as she scrubbed the end of Nathan's box spring. A droplet landed between her eyes and rolled down her nose. With a rubber-gloved hand she smeared it, hating the smell of it, hating the very idea that she had to be doing this. Her head itched under its tight covering of towel and plastic hood. She shuddered. No, she told herself sternly. Do not scratch. There is no need.

"Mom!" Katie's voice, shrieking from downstairs, startled her. "I'm hungry!"

"Me too!" That was Nathan, with his voice far too big for a seven-year-old. Of course Nathan was perpetually hungry. Maybe to feed that voice. He'd had a sandwich after she picked him up at school at three.

"Just a minute," she called. "I'm almost done."

With her teeth she peeled back the cuff of an orange rubber glove to look at her watch. Lord, it was past dinnertime. The kids were hungry, and she had nothing prepared, and she'd been lying. She was not almost done. When she'd finished Nathan's bed, there was still her own to do, as well as the sofa and chairs in both the family and living rooms. That would all wait until after dinner; but dinner would wait until she had Nathan's room back together.

"You can each have a banana," she shouted to the children before she stood and wrestled the bed out from the wall. Then, crawling along the floor, the long, baggy legs of her white plastic painter's suit unrolling and tripping her, she scrubbed the back side of the box spring. Should she attempt to turn it over and do the bottom?

She tried to recall what the shampoo bottle had said. The little critters could live for some time away from the human body. Clothing, mattresses, bed linens, pillows—all had to be cleaned. Mattresses, yes, but had they even mentioned box springs? Probably they thought it went without saying. *Reinfestation is common*.

"Tell me about it," she muttered.

She shuddered again. And itched.

The doorbell rang. "Mom!" Nathan's raucous voice bellowed again.

"Just a minute!" Kat squirmed on her knees and tried to get out from behind the bed, which she could move no farther out from the wall due to the mattress lying on the floor. Oh, heavens! What if she'd put that clean, disinfected mattress right on a nest of the evil little things? Did they live in the carpet too? She'd vacuumed, but was that enough? Should she have shampooed the rugs before she did the beds?

Oh, hell, what she should have done was call an exterminator. But she'd been too embarrassed even to consider telling another living soul what had happened, not only to her children, but to herself. She'd driven clear across town to a strange drugstore to buy the shampoo.

She clenched her teeth on another shudder of pure disgust and forced herself not to scratch. She was clean. She was squeaky-clean. She knew that! She just wished she could convince her skin.

The doorbell rang again. She also wished she had time for a nervous breakdown. She didn't want to see anyone right now.

"Mom! Dad's here!"

"Seize the moment," Kat muttered to herself as heavy footsteps sounded in the hall, along with a deep laughing voice and two excited childish ones. "Nobody ever has *time* for a nervous breakdown. They simply happen. Lie down on the floor. Close your eyes. Sink deep into a state of unconsciousness. You may twitch a little, and drool."

"Mom? Are you praying?" Nathan asked.

"For my immediate disappearance, I'm sure." That was her ex-husband.

Kat's eyes popped open and ran smack into the power of Rand's gaze. Dammit, she wasn't lying on the floor. She wasn't in a deep state of unconsciousness. No kindly ambulance attendants were going to strap her onto a stretcher and take her away from all this. She was still kneeling on the floor behind her son's bed, still held a scrub brush in her hand, and her head still itched unbearably.

She peeled off a glove, untied the strings under her chin, shoved back the hood, reached under her towel, and scratched. She might also, she thought, start twitching soon.

She refused to drool.

This was the closest she'd been to Rand for just a shade more than two years. He hadn't changed much. There was some gray at his temples, a line or two around his mouth; the crow's-feet were a tad deeper. The cleft in his chin was still just off center.

It was fear that one of the kids might tell him why she was cleaning that dried her mouth and dampened her palms. That was all. Besides, it had been a rough week all around. No wonder her hands were shaking the way they did. It had nothing to do with Rand's presence. Not on a personal level.

"Hello, Kat," he said. "How have you been?"

"Since you ask," she said, "lousy." It was all she could do to suppress an hysterical urge to laugh at her intentional, secret pun.

He smiled faintly. "Were you praying?"

"No." She turned to her son. "Nathan, how many times have I told you, you do not answer the door. You come and get me, and I answer the door."

"But, Mom! It's *Dad*! He's not a stranger."

"That's not your mother's fault," Rand said. His hands, looking absurdly large, held one of Katie's, one of Nathan's. His gaze, however, held Kat's.

She refused to look away. "That's not fair." He was the one who'd spent more time away from home during their marriage than he'd spent with his family. And then he'd had the gall to go ballistic if she had to work late on one of the few evenings he'd managed to spend in this house.

His eyes were as black as sin, as they'd always been. His brows, straight and thick, raised upward. He shrugged. "If you say so."

She levered herself to her feet. "I say so."

"All right. I didn't come to discuss that." He didn't say what he had come to discuss, though. He merely continued to look at her while she stood on the far side of Nathan's bed dressed like a clown.

Kat's resentment grew. It gnawed at her insides. It filled her chest. It made her throat ache. It made her feel like crying. A powerful emotion, resentment.

Rand's voice, deep, resonant, capable of the angriest roar, the tenderest croon, and every nuance in between, held amusement when he spoke again. "Nice . . . er . . . jumpsuit, Kat. New fashion?"

Resentment turned to outright fury. "Oh, shut up! I don't require sarcasm from you, Randall." Guiltily, she looked at the children, whom she had forbidden to say "Shut up."

Nathan and Katie gazed back at her with identical, round dark eyes fringed with the same outrageously luxurious lashes as their father's. Kat lowered her gaze and chewed on her bottom lip before looking at her ex-husband again. "What do you want, Rand?" With sickening suddenness it occurred to her that maybe, over the weekend, the kids had distributed their largesse to him, and he was here to confront her for child neglect. She bit her lip, staring at him. No, surely not. He didn't appear to be itching. Or even angry.

He eyed the stripped-down bed, the brush, and the bucket of disinfectant. "Finished?"

Kat struggled out from behind the bed. She nodded, then ground her back teeth together when he bent and lifted the mattress with supreme ease, settling it exactly square on the box spring.

"You're strong, Daddy."

Kat clenched her jaw even tighter at Katie's googly-eyed admiration, even though she told herself a five-year-old girl was entitled to idolize her daddy.

Rand scooped Katie up in one arm and made a muscle with the other. "You like a strong guy, huh? There you go. Feel that." Katie did, grunting and biting her lower lip as she tried to make a dent in the solid flesh. Kat knew how impossible it was. As impossible as making a dent in Rand's solid will. Or his solid head.

"Can I try, Dad?"

"Sure, Nathan." Rand crouched and let Nathan feel his muscles, then admired the boy's bunched biceps and assured him that in thirty years, he'd have the same kind of strength as his father.

"Me too?" asked Katie.

Rand smiled at her, then flicked a glance at Kat. "You'll have . . . different kinds of strengths, punkin. But they'll be even more powerful, believe me."

"Mom, when can we eat?" Nathan asked. "Can Dad stay?"

"No, he can't." Kat knew she sounded ungracious, but she didn't think she could handle seeing Rand at the table with her children. All that . . . resentment, or whatever it was, would choke her. "I haven't got anything ready for dinner."

Nathan was incensed. "Why not? Whatcha been doing?"

Kat ground her teeth together again. That wasn't fair either. She'd worked her butt off trying to make their home clean and safe to live in, and all she got from the kids was, "I'm hungry and why isn't dinner on the table?" Yet Rand waltzed in, lifted one mattress, and got praised to the skies.

It had cost her one fingernail to get Katie's mattress off her bed, and three more to get it back on properly. She'd likely lose a whole handful of them doing her own bed.

"Hey, guys, there are treats in my jacket pockets," Rand said. "The left side is Katie's, the right is Nathan's. Why don't you go downstairs and see—"

"Dammit, Rand," Kat interrupted. She pulled her other glove off with an audible snap and dropped it beside the bucket. "No treats before dinner."

"Not edible treats. Go on." He shooed the children out of the room and leaned in the doorway, looking at Kat. She swept her gaze over him as she unzipped the plastic suit and shrugged her shoulders free so she could shove the garment down past her hips.

His jeans were old, faded, and tight. His short-sleeved shirt was so soft from washings, it clung to his chest and arms. He required no fist to make his biceps appear round and hard, drawing the sleeves tight across them. He needed a haircut. But then, when hadn't he needed a haircut? He always forgot, unless she reminded him. He'd said he liked her to remind him. It made him feel as if he was important to her.

"What do you want?" she asked again, sitting on the end of Nathan's bed to continue getting rid of the suit.

"To talk."

She kicked her legs out of confinement. "Did they cut off your phone?"

He shouldered himself erect in the doorway. "No, but I didn't want to talk on the phone, and if I'd called, you'd have said you were too busy to see me."

"That," she said tersely, "is the truth."

He nodded. "I can see that. Spring cleaning?" he asked, eyeing the plastic suit. "Or did you have a nuclear spill?"

Relief made her momentarily dizzy enough to ignore that little dig about her appearance. She was only grateful that the kids hadn't told him why she was in a cleaning frenzy. She bent forward to ease the elastic cuffs of the suit over the heels of her running shoes.

"I thought you had someone in to do the heavy stuff," Rand continued.

"Not this time."

"Kat . . ." He frowned as he hesitated, clearly and uncharacteristically unsure for a moment. He scuffed one foot in the carpet, then batted at the tail of a model plane hanging from the ceiling, setting it swinging. "Kat, is it because you're short of money? You know you only have to ask if . . ." He let it trail off.

Despite herself, Kat was touched by the question and the offer. But then, Rand had never been ungenerous. Not with money, anyway. "I'm not short of money. Sometimes I like to clean things up for myself."

Mercifully, he didn't dispute that but surprised the hell out of her by saying, "Tell me what's left to be done. I'll help, then we can talk."

She lifted her head sharply and stared at him as she kicked her feet free.

"You? Do housework?"

He looked at her levelly. "I do housework, Kat."

She picked up her bucket and gloves and draped the painter's suit over her arm. "Since when?"

A hint of rose stained the dark skin on his high cheekbones. "Since I discovered that it doesn't get done all by itself."

"My," she said, slipping past him. "Such an epiphany that must have been. It's a wonder the earth didn't open up and swallow you."

"If it had," he said, following her as she headed toward the stairs, "I wouldn't be here offering to help you."

"What a trade-off. I'm glad I wasn't asked to choose."

"I'll let that pass because I know you're beat. You always got bitchy when you were tired." Then, as if he couldn't help himself, he added, "You were tired a lot. But the offer stands."

"If you're saying I was always bitchy, it was because I was always trying to do everything myself. My job, raising the kids, looking after the house."

"You had no need to work," he retorted. "I earned enough to give you and the kids everything you needed."

Her temper threatened to overwhelm her. "*I* had a need!" He'd never understood that. "There were factors beyond money at issue and—" Kat broke off, her teeth clacking together audibly. She drew a deep breath, let it out very slowly, unclenched her jaw, and felt the ache of anger begin to ease its grip around her head. How many times had they been over that? Nothing had changed. Nothing would change. Nothing could change. Discussing it was pointless.

Suddenly, perversely, she was tempted to accept his offer, to throw the hot plastic garment, the sweaty rubber gloves, at him and tell him to go scrub her bed, just to see the look on his face. But not for the world would she admit to him that the job needed to be done, or why.

He'd laugh. That was one thing she couldn't take, Rand Waddell laughing at her.

"Offer rejected," she said, stomping down the flight of four stairs to the main floor. She continued through the kitchen to the laundry room, where she emptied the bucket down the tub. "Go away and play, Rand," she said, hearing him follow right behind her. "You just saw the kids last weekend."

"I know. It's you I want to see."

She glared at him over her shoulder. "After two years? Why?"

He gave her a long, level look to remind her of the times he'd asked to see her—and been refused. "Now who's not being fair?"

She closed her eyes and turned her head. She heard the children playing in the family room. Nathan was making motor sounds, which meant that Rand had brought him an airplane. Nathan had an aircraft fixation. Katie was talking in a high, squeaky voice alternating with a deep, gruff one. That could mean anything from a new storybook to a pair of plastic dinosaurs.

Rand was right. She was the one who'd refused adamantly to see him. The way she felt now, all churned up and tight and hell, let's face it, sick with an "Achy, Breaky Heart" feeling that made her eyes sting and her throat hurt, she'd been right to refuse. Seeing him was hard, remembering the way it had been, the way she'd thought it would be forever. And the ways in which she had failed.

She shoved her hands into the gloves again, turned on the hot water, and washed the bucket, wrinkling her nose as heat increased the pungency of the disinfectant.

"I haven't got time to talk to you," she said, concentrating on wiping out the bucket with a clean, dry cloth. She stared at it as if she might find a solution to all her troubles within its red plastic depths. "I have to fix something for the kids to eat."

"They can't be starving. They were both eating bananas when I came in."

"I know. But it's past dinnertime."

"All right. Tell me what you want done. I can help with it."

"No," she said, and was surprised to see disappointment in his eyes. She sighed silently. They were his kids, too, and he loved them as much as she did. It wouldn't hurt her to let him have them for a few extra hours. Besides, then she could finish the cleaning before bedtime.

"If you really want to help," she said, "take them out to McDonald's and feed them. Just have them back by seven-thirty. There's school tomorrow."

Rand picked up the painter's suit she'd dropped on the floor and hung it on a hook on the wall. "If I did that, you'd go back to your scrubbing."

She met his gaze. "Yes, I would."

"And I don't want you to."

"Rand, what you want and do not want are no longer prime considerations in my life."

"As if they ever were!"

She opened her mouth to mention how hard she'd tried, but he held up a hand to stop her. "I know, I know. Don't bother saying it. Just take a look at yourself. Your hands are shaking; your face is pale. You need food too. And to sit down. If you did that, we could talk. Why don't you admit it? You're too tired to do whatever else you'd planned to do this evening."

Her temper, which she'd been holding on to with difficulty, flared again. "Dammit, why do you keep pushing me? I said I don't want to talk. To you. About anything but the kids. And then only when necessary. And the phone will do for that."

"This is about the kids."

His exaggerated air of forebearance grated on her nerves. She slammed the bucket down on top of the washer and glared at him. "All right! *What* about the kids?" Dammit, didn't he know how hard this was for her? Or was it simply that he didn't care?

Oh, come on, Kat! Of course he doesn't care! Why would you expect him to?

"Why did you advertise for a live-in nanny?" he asked.

She blinked stupidly for a moment or two, so unexpected was the question.

"How did you know I did that?" Dumb question. Of course the kids had told him.

He shrugged, showing off his shoulders. Rand was proud of those shoulders. Once, she'd thought they were pretty great herself. Not now, though, of course. Except maybe in a very . . . detached and impersonal way. Nice to see from a distance, but bearing no relationship to reality.

"Nate mentioned it. He's not what you'd call keen on the idea, Kat."

"I know." She fixed her gaze on his midriff to take her mind off his shoulders. Was that a hint of a spare tire there? Yes! By golly, yes, it was. She had to fight to suppress a pleased smile. So Mr. Wonderful was beginning to show his thirty-seven years. That kind of reality she could appreciate, being thirty-four herself and becoming increasingly aware of the effects of gravity.

"I'm aware of Nathan's objections," she said, forcing herself to meet his gaze again. "But I'm the adult in this household, Rand. I bear the responsibility, and I have to make the decisions."

He swung into attack mode. "I bear some of that responsibility, Katherine. How can you think of bringing a stranger to live in your home with you? With my children?"

Katherine. He only called her that when he was annoyed.

She grimaced, annoyed herself with his attitude. "Really, *Randall*. People move in with strangers all the time. Sometimes they call it marriage."

His eyes narrowed as they always had when she reminded him that they'd known each other less than three months when they got married. Randlike, though, he stuck to the subject he'd chosen. "You have no right to make a unilateral decision on something like that without consulting me."

She stared. "Of course I do! I'm the custodial parent, and I'm not going to hire a pedophile, for goodness sake! I'm also the one who's going to have to live with the nanny. Why should you be consulted? Or even concerned? After all, you trusted me to care for them—unilaterally—every time you were . . . out of town."

He didn't respond to the tonal quotes she'd put around the last three words. It seemed there were things that he, too, refused to touch. "That was different," he said. "I was leaving my children with their mother. And I should have been consulted about this. I am concerned because I'm their father."

"Well, now's a fine time to think of that," she said, knowing full well he was right on both counts. Before he could rise to the bait, she added quickly, "I need someone here for the kids, Rand, and I need that person soon. Like yesterday. There wasn't time to consult you. I simply had to act."

"Why? What's wrong with the day care they've been attending since Jenny—"

He broke off and looked down at his feet.

Kat swallowed the unexpected stab of grief that tore into her throat. It was, she realized suddenly, grief Rand must share, must have shared these past four months since Jenny and Karl Morrison, their dearest friends, had died along with their three children in a traffic accident.

She and Rand had never spoken of it together.

It seemed strange that this was the first time she'd acknowledged that he'd be grieving, too, and like her, doing it all alone. She didn't believe for a minute that any of his girlfriends could possibly understand what losing Jenny, Karl, and their children meant to him.

"Why do you need a nanny?" he asked finally, glancing up. She saw a residue of pain in his eyes. "What's wrong with their day-care?"

"They weren't . . . happy there." Or safe, events had proved. "Until I find someone to care for them here, I'm taking vacation time, sick days, whatever it takes, even a leave of absence from my job if I need it. This whole thing came to a head"—oh, she loved these little plays on words—"just as spring break started."

And the situation continued, though the kids had gone back to school the past Monday. With any luck, after today, the problem would be well and truly eradicated.

She had only one more louse to get out of her hair.

"And now that I've explained, Rand, perhaps you'd either take the kids out for dinner or go by yourself. But I, as you can see, have work to do. We wouldn't want our new nanny seeing a dirty house, now, would we?"

Her reward was the tightening of his lips, the narrowing of his eyes. He hated it when she spoke to him as if he were a recalcitrant child. Good. If he hated her half as much as she hated him, then he wouldn't want to spend another second in her company.

"Good-bye, Rand."

His smile—no, wrong word, Kat decided—irked her. It was too much like a smirk. "That," he said, "is why I didn't phone. Do you know you just 'hung up' on me, Katherine, saying good-bye in that final manner?" He smirked again. "But it doesn't work when we're face-to-face. I'm still here, in case you didn't notice."

She compressed her lips. "I noticed. All right. What do you want from me?"

"A better, more comprehensive explanation. I want to know a hell of a lot more about this entire scheme of yours before I give my assent to it."

"All right!" She puffed out an impatient breath. "This is what's happened so far: I've interviewed several women from three different agencies. None of them was suitable, so I decided to go it alone, try the papers. I'm sure the perfect woman is out there, looking for a family who needs her as much as we do. Not everyone likes to work through an agency. And I have a lot to offer a potential employee, not just a private room, but a fully furnished basement suite she can live in."

She rinsed the gloves under the tap, turned them inside out, and sprinkled talcum over them. "Maybe it was providence that I didn't bother to find a new tenant after Mrs. Gold left. It makes more sense to put a nanny in the apartment. Her wages, combined with the lost revenue from the suite, will still likely be close to the cost of day care, possibly even less."

Rand frowned. "How much do you figure on paying her?"

Kat told him, adding, "Since she's getting her housing provided, the agencies I spoke to all felt it was more than adequate. And it's about a third of what I pay for day care."

"I didn't know day care cost that much."

She could have told him there was a whole lot he didn't know about raising children, but she managed to bite her tongue as she shook the powder can harder.

The scent of baby powder invaded the room. "I like that smell," Rand said.

She did too. It reminded her of times past, when the world was a different place, when love was young and new and everything seemed possible. A lifetime ago.

She lifted her head and discovered him much too close to her, leaving her no room to turn without touching him. "I remember coming home to it." His voice was soft, sad, she thought. "It always seemed so . . . warm. So welcoming."

Before his melancholy could get to her, she shouldered past him, then tossed him the pink-and-white
can. "Great. Take it with you. Sprinkle it on your latest
girlfriend." She strode from the room.

In the kitchen she scowled at the range hood. For
a man who liked the scent of baby powder, he'd stayed
single a surprisingly long time since their divorce.

"Kat . . ." She tensed as he spoke behind her.

"Kat, there's something . . . I . . ."

As his voice trailed off, she heard the frown she
refused to turn and see. All at once, her heart began
hammering too hard in her chest, making her dizzy.
Was he about to get married again? Was that really
what he'd wanted to talk to her about, what he hadn't
wanted to say over the phone?

She clenched her hands into tight fists as she steeled
herself for whatever might come.

Nothing did. He remained silent. She couldn't stand
it. She swung around and looked at him. "What?" she
almost shouted. "What is it you really want, Rand?"

"Want? What makes you so sure I want something?" He tossed the powder can from hand to hand,
outwardly calm and relaxed. His face was bland, his
eyes appeared to be hiding nothing, but . . . Oh, Lord,
she knew him well enough to be fully aware that he
was being cagey. Maybe he hadn't asked the woman
to marry him yet but planned to soon and didn't want
to mention it to anyone else first, for fear of jinxing his
hopes.

And what about her hopes? Not for herself, of
course, but for her kids. What if he married someone completely inappropriate? Someone they hated,
someone who hated them? Who wouldn't be nice to

them? It didn't seem right, that a man could remarry and the mother of his children had no say in the matter at all, even though the kids would have to live with that woman part of the time.

"You're here," she said. "To me, that suggests you want something."

"Maybe what I want is simply to be here."

Yeah. Right. Biting her lip, she snatched a box of macaroni-and-cheese mix out of a cupboard and stared at the directions printed on its back, as if she hadn't prepared the same thing a hundred times.

Dear God! What if he was trying to tell her he wanted the kids? What if he and his new wife applied for custody on the grounds that Kat wasn't providing the kind of clean, stable home the children needed?

How would it sound in court? "Your Honor, my clients, Mr. and Mrs. Waddell, petition for the custody of Mr. Waddell's children by his first marriage on the grounds that their mother put them in an unclean day-care center, where they became infested with head lice."

She stifled a groan and crouched by a cupboard, gripping her self-control far harder than she clasped the cooking pot that her hands locked around.

Rand clenched his teeth as Kat squatted and pulled a large pot out of a cupboard. Her knees bent, her thighs flexed, her buttocks pulled the fabric of her jeans tight. Involuntarily, his hand curved as if to stroke over that sweet, familiar shape. Lord, but he wanted to touch her, wanted to put his hands on her waist and pull her to her feet.

She stood, even as he took a hesitant step toward her, and swung around to fill the pot with water. That done, she set it onto the stove, half turning toward him as she reached out to switch on a burner. She didn't meet his gaze, though. Her face wore a closed, shuttered look, and she'd squared her jaw the way she always did when she didn't like what he had to say.

What wasn't to like? He hadn't said anything yet. She couldn't possibly have any inkling of what he was about to suggest.

He knew he was going to get a battle from her. In a way he was looking forward to it. Even a battle with Kat would be more fun than this terrible silence she'd imposed on him, her total refusal to listen to anything he had to say.

He'd changed. He knew that. He'd grown and learned and saw things entirely differently now. The thing was, she didn't know that about him, and unless he made this plan work, she'd never know it. He'd never have a chance to show her that things could really be different.

Except, one thing hadn't changed. He still wanted her with a kind of pain that wouldn't quit.

He put a hand on her shoulder, turning her around. "Kat, please let me talk, even if you don't want to talk to me. There might be another solution, one you haven't considered."

Kat stared at his left hand, at his fingers wrapped over the sleeve of her gray sweatshirt. His wide gold wedding band glimmered dully in the light. If he was going to get married again, wouldn't he have taken that off?

Dammit, she didn't *care* what his plans were! And she didn't care to have him touch her. She jerked free and backed up three steps. His arm fell to his side.

"What solution?" she asked.

"I don't want you to hire a nanny at all. I want to move back into the house so I can be here to look after the kids when you're not."

TWO

"What?" Kat's voice was a squeak of disbelief.

Rand saw her face go paler than before, except for a pair of bright red marks on her cheekbones. They were reminiscent of a bout she'd had with pneumonia, and a day he'd rather not remember.

He clamped his teeth so hard, his jaws ached. Once, he'd seen that day as the beginning of the end. Now, he knew better. That had simply been the day that he'd recognized, beyond doubt, that there was no point in trying any longer. Yet for all that, it was an end he'd never fully accepted.

Hell! He should have led up to this by a more circuitous route, but he'd managed to say it and wasn't about to back down.

"You heard me, Katherine. I was going to ask for the spare bedroom, but since you mean to put a nanny in the basement suite, I can see it's a much better idea for me to live there."

"April Fool's Day was yesterday, Rand."

"This is no joke."

"You can't be serious!"

"I am. Dead serious."

She shook her head, her hair bouncing and gleaming. He wanted to capture a handful of it. A handful of sunsets.

"Rand . . ." She sounded frantic. "I thought I'd made myself clear. I need someone to live here *all* the time. Someone who can walk the kids to school in the morning, pick Katie up after kindergarten, bring her home for lunch, and entertain her for the rest of the afternoon until it's time to go and get Nathan. I need someone who's ready at a moment's notice to take over in the evening if I can't get home from work on time, or if I have to go back to the office."

"I realize that. I will be available at a moment's notice."

Her glare was as scathing as her words. "Hah! That'll be the day! You couldn't even make yourself available on either of their due dates! I'm surprised you managed to be there for their concep—"

Kat broke off, biting her tongue as Nathan and Katie appeared in the doorway. She wanted to run to them, to put them between her and Rand, but they seemed not to see her. Nathan's eyes, big and dark and pleading, were on his father as he said, "Dad, can you come and show me how to make my glider do loop-the-loops?"

Rand crossed the room in three paces, repositioned the glider's wings in the slot on its back, and said, "There, try that. In the other room."

"Come and play."

"Yes, Daddy. Then you can read me my new story."

"Later, sweetheart." Rand smiled at his daughter. "Your mommy and I have things to talk about now."

"No, we don't," Kat said quickly, finally overcoming the shock that had held her almost immobile since Rand's incredible statement. "Why don't you entertain the kids while I get their dinner ready? Go on. You're always complaining you don't get enough time with them."

"And I don't get any time with you," he said.

"You don't need time with me! You—"

"Nate, later, okay, Son?" he said as Nathan continued to hover in the doorway. "I promise, I'll show you all the tricks your plane can do. Just give me a few minutes alone with your mother."

Nathan shrugged, taking himself and his glider away. His sister followed.

"You should be with them," Kat said, aware of the note of desperation in her voice. "Not with me. And if you're worried about my choosing the right nanny, when I select one, I'll send her to you for your final approval."

"That's not what I want. I told you what I want, Kat."

"But . . . But that's . . . preposterous!" she sputtered. "You . . . I . . . ." She shook her head rapidly again. "Forget it! I'll hire a nanny as planned. You just make yourself available for whatever foreign assignment comes your way, the way you always have."

Rand watched her as she turned away to check the water in the pot. Foreign assignment? Brother, was she out of date! "I don't go out of town anymore, Kat."

She spun back. "Since when?"

"For a long time." He tightened his jaw against the wrench of pain her question brought. Didn't she care enough to ask the kids *anything* about him? He demanded and got a full update on her doings whenever they were with him.

He ran both hands into his hair, massaging his scalp. No. Of course she didn't care enough to ask. She didn't care, period. But he'd known that. What he hoped for now was to change it.

She opened the fridge and took out a couple of carrots, which she scrubbed vigorously under the tap.

Likely, he thought, the subject of what he did had never come up between her and the kids. At the time of their breakup, Nathan hadn't been quite five, and Katie still under three. Neither of them would have known enough to tell her that Daddy didn't go away on assignments anymore.

But couldn't Kat have figured it out for herself? Had he ever missed one of his weekends with the kids? Didn't she notice that he was available a hell of a lot more often for them than the two weekends a month the family-court judge had stipulated?

His throat tightened. She had more important considerations than a discarded husband.

"I only accept assignments," he said finally, "that can be done without interfering with my time with the kids."

She gave him a thoughtful glance over her shoulder. "That's a change."

"*I've* changed."

This time her look was clearly skeptical. It irked him to the point that he backed away from his intent to tell her that immediately after she'd left him, he'd applied for a different position at the paper in order to stay in town.

"If you'd agreed to see me," he said, "to talk to me for more than three minutes any time during the past couple of years, you'd know that already."

Her shrug let him know that even if she believed him, it changed nothing for her. She didn't ask for further details. She didn't want them. He paid child support and half the mortgage, but she earned enough as a statistician with a research outfit that she likely could have done it all without him.

He wished he'd grown and changed enough that her working didn't still bother him so much. He wanted her to need him, but Kat had never needed him as completely as he'd needed her. Not in the ways that mattered.

He watched her rummage in the fridge again, coming up with a cucumber and a head of lettuce, thumping them down onto a cutting board that covered one of the white porcelain sinks. He pulled out a stool from under the bar that separated the kitchen from the dining area. It still gave him a deep pleasure to watch her preparing a meal.

Her hands, long-fingered, pale-skinned, with neatly trimmed nails—and wearing both of the rings he had given her—worked efficiently. He remembered how they'd felt, massaging his back when he was in pain, strong, rhythmic, healing. He also recalled them soft and trembling on his body as he aroused her, then firm and insistent as her passion grew. Aggressive. Demanding. In that way, she had needed him. . . .

He jerked his mind off that track. Irritated with himself more than with her, he said, "Dammit, Katherine, will you talk to me?" If she talked, maybe he wouldn't think.

She glanced at him and shrugged again, the motion disturbing the tumble of strawberry-blond curls, tousled from being wrapped in a towel. He remembered, too, the way her hair had felt against his chest, his stomach, his thighs. He clenched his teeth. Damn! Maybe he'd been lucky, these past couple of years, that she'd arranged never to be in the same room with him.

"We did talk," she said, peeling the cucumber with sharp, angry motions. "You made a suggestion that doesn't bear discussion. What more is there to say? Unless you want to talk about what kind of a nanny I—we—should hire."

"All right, let's talk about that," he said. "And about why you think that's a better idea than mine."

Agreeing to talk about it didn't mean he'd given up. But maybe he should let her have some time to play with the notion of his moving into the suite.

"You said Katie and Nathan weren't 'happy' in their day-care. Apart from grieving over losing Jen, they've seemed happy enough to me. So, explain."

"I thought I had. I don't think after-school day-care was the right solution."

"And *I* don't think some strange woman living in is the right solution. Let's work on that one for a few minutes."

She looked at him, then sighed and added another measure of water to the pot. She took a second package of macaroni and cheese from the cupboard and set it beside the first.

He was, he guessed, going to be offered dinner after all. He hated macaroni and cheese, but that didn't matter. He wanted to go hug her and tell her thanks. It had been a long time since he'd sat in this house over a meal with his family. It had been even longer since he'd hugged his wife. Ex-wife.

"It simply wasn't working out," she repeated. "For them or for me. Sometimes I have to work late."

"Yeah. I remember."

"When I work late," she said, ignoring his comment, "it means calling someone to pick up the kids at day-care, bringing them home, and staying with them. Having someone live in would provide more continuity in their lives—no strange baby-sitters. With someone here to get her there and back, Katie could take the ballet lessons she wants so badly. It's the ideal solution, Rand."

"What about their mother being here for them?" he asked before he could stop himself. "Talk about your ideal solutions."

She slammed the paring knife down on the cutting board and faced him, eyes snapping. "Rand—"

"All right, all right." He held up a hand to forestall her tirade. "I'm sorry. That was uncalled for."

"You bet it was!"

He suppressed a sigh. "Kat, dreams die hard."

"It was your dream, never mine. We both knew our dreams differed. We ignored that. We took the risk, and we lost."

He nodded. "I know, but I still can't help wishing things had been different."

After a moment she nodded as well. "Me too," she said softly, her blue-gray eyes somber as she met his gaze. "But things aren't different, Rand. Didn't you used to tell me to play the cards I'd been dealt? Did you ever once consider taking your own advice?"

He stared down at the scuffed toes of his running shoes as he sat on the stool, legs shoved out in front of him.

Yeah, he thought. He'd always reminded her that she knew about his job before they married, that she'd once thought it romantic and thrilling to get midnight phone calls from exotic foreign places. She was right, though, and he shouldn't try to make out that the game had gone wrong because of a misdeal on her part. He, too, had known what to expect right from the beginning.

He watched her chopping vegetables, saying nothing. After all, what was there to say? He'd married an independent-minded, self-confident woman who had plans for her future, so it shouldn't have come as such a surprise when staying home hadn't been enough for her. But it had left him feeling cheated of something valuable, and it had hurt. He'd wanted children, wanted them raised in a loving, cohesive family, in a real home where the mother was available for them every minute of every day and night. He'd wanted that for as long as he could remember.

More than that, he'd wanted someone warm to come home to himself. He'd dreamed of welcoming arms, a happy smile, not a note propped on the counter saying that the kids were next door and Kat would be home by nine.

The kids. He leaned back against the breakfast bar, watching Kat work, listening to Katie and Nate playing in the family room. He turned his head, glancing down into the sunken room, and saw the pair of them grappling on the floor in front of the TV. It almost tempted him to go and join them.

They were fine, well-adjusted little people, and Kat was doing a great job, despite doing most of it alone. Sure, he'd planned to be an important figure in his children's lives, and he had been, as much as his profession permitted. Ironically, he'd spent almost as much time with them since the divorce than he had before. He'd known for a long time that all of them needed more than they were getting. Himself. The kids. And Kat.

He swung his gaze back to her.

Until Nathan had told him what Kat planned, he'd seen no practical way of changing the status quo short of going for custody, which he would never do. Whatever her faults, Kat loved the kids and would be devastated to lose them.

He'd been pretty well devastated himself, when she had left him, packed her things and theirs, moved out. He'd found them living in a too-small apartment, which she'd said was all she could afford. He'd been unable to let them live in such surroundings without feeling like a total failure, and he'd moved out of this house so they could return.

Failures . . . His life had been comprised of them. He looked up again, catching Kat's gaze on him. She didn't look away immediately.

He smiled, and for a moment he thought he detected a hint of a smile in her eyes. It was gone before he could be sure. But he wanted her smiles. He wanted her laughter. He wanted to share the joy she had once taken in life.

He wanted it all to come together again, and nothing she said would convince him that this wasn't the perfect opportunity.

He tried again. "If you want someone who loves the kids occupying that suite, who could be better than their own father?"

Kat sighed as she selected a larger knife from the wooden-block holder Rand had given her one year for Christmas. "Rand, I don't understand why you seem set on making difficulties over this issue. I don't want *you* living in this house. I want a nanny."

"I'm not set on making difficulties. I just don't like the idea of your hiring a strange person, bringing her into my children's home, leaving her alone with them for hours at a time."

Kat set the salad bowl into the right-hand sink and swept chopped vegetables into it from the board. As she tossed them to mix in the shredded carrot, she frowned. It was, of course, his right to know who cared for the children.

As she rinsed her hands, she flashed on the thought she'd had about his getting to choose their stepmother without any input from her. Wasn't her determination to hire a nanny the same kind of thing?

"I'm their mother," she said, reluctant to concede any point too easily. "Don't you trust my judgment?"

"I trust your judgment, Kat."

The pot lid rattled as the water came to a boil. Rand stood and added the two packages of macaroni to the water. Kat stared, biting her lower lip as she watched Rand stir the pasta. It was such a novel sight, her ex-husband at work in the kitchen. When he'd been her husband, he'd thought the kitchen was a place he was called to when dinner was ready, or maybe to repair a dripping faucet.

He set the lid back on at an angle and adjusted the heat. "What was wrong with the nannies you interviewed?"

She outlined the variety of failings she'd found in the women, concluding with an indignant gripe about one. Rand grinned at the outrage in her tone. He'd always enjoyed Kat's passionate nature. She looked so cool and ignited so readily.

His grin faded as she went on, leaving him with a scowl on his face. She'd been right to reject every one of those women. His determination hardened to save his children from this screwy idea of their mother's.

"I want someone," she concluded, "not just to look after the kids, but to love them the way Jenny did." Her voice cracked. Her pointed chin trembled for just an instant.

Rand nodded, his gaze holding hers. He saw the sheen of unshed tears in her eyes. "Yeah, I know. I miss her too. And Karl. And their kids."

As if ashamed of showing any weakness in front of him, she stiffened her shoulders and swung away. Of course she didn't want comfort from him. She didn't want anything from him. His wanting anything from her was as futile as wishing for Jenny and Karl to come back from their graves.

Jenny had been the kids' baby-sitter from the time Kat went back to work when Katie was five months old. She'd lived next door with her husband and three children, had adored both Nathan and Katie, and they had idolized her.

The four of them, Jenny and Karl, Kat and Rand, had been close through all those early years. Even after the divorce, the Morrisons had remained friends to both Rand and Kat. Their instant deaths when a drunk driver had run into them during a high-speed flight from the police had been a vicious blow.

"Kat . . ." he began. "That day, at the funeral, I wanted to—"

The macaroni water boiled over with a loud hiss and a gout of steam. Kat dived for it at the same moment Rand did. They collided in midkitchen.

Kat froze as Rand's hands clamped over her shoulders. For an instant she couldn't move as he held her, steadying her. When he jerked away, he left behind two patches of heat on her shoulders, another two from the sizzle of his chest against her breasts, and one where her left hand had landed on that incipient spare tire of his.

Love handles. The term popped up from nowhere, snatching her breath away. She forced herself to breathe and smelled the familiar scent of his aftershave. It hung around her for a moment like an aura.

He set the lid aside and stirred the boil down in the pot.

The boil in her continued unabated.

She dragged a stool under herself before her knocking knees became apparent.

"All I want," she said, when she trusted her voice enough to speak, "is for the kids to be as safe and happy and well-looked-after as they were with Jen."

"Don't you think they would be, with me?"

She shrugged and slid off the stool, going back to her salad making. As she added mushroom slices and tomato wedges artistically around the tossed greens, she wondered why she was taking the trouble. The answer disturbed her so much, she refused to acknowledge it.

"Kat?"

She flicked a glance at him. "I know you love them, Rand, but that's simply not enough. I want someone who'll devote her life to their care."

He nodded, fixing her with a pointed stare. "That's all I ever wanted, too, Kat."

She paused in the act of sprinkling bacon bits over the salad. "And you married the wrong woman. One who wasn't content to do that."

He leaned on the counter, looking at her. "I wanted you."

She shook her head, appalled to find tears stinging her eyes again. She busied herself combining the ingredients for the cheese sauce. "No, Rand. You wanted what you thought I should be, the fantasy you'd created out of your . . . need. When you tried to fit me into the mold you thought meant 'wife and mother,' I didn't fit. The *reality* of me didn't make you happy."

"What makes you so sure you're not looking for the same kind of fantasy in hiring a nanny? You want from her what you claim is all I really wanted from you, a woman to stay home and clean house, bake bread, and breed."

She looked up as she set a colander in the sink. "I do not," she said dryly, "want my nanny to breed."

Rand grinned as he picked up a fork, snitched a bit of macaroni from the boiling water, and blew on it to cool it. "No. But you want her to love your children, to raise them to be the kind of adults you can be proud of." Still blowing against the heat, he gingerly bit the morsel of pasta, testing it for doneness.

"I plan to do the raising myself," she said. "With her help."

He took the pot of macaroni off the stove and poured it into the colander. "I plan to have a lot of input in their rearing as well," he said, as if to remind her that they were his children too. "And it would be a lot easier for me to do it if I were in the same house."

Kat avoided his dark gaze by running water over the pasta. Dammit, what he said made sense. Too much sense. And the kids would love it. But she . . . She'd hate it. She'd have to listen to his phone ringing, listen to the murmur of his voice as he made dates with his girlfriends. Then the kids would go downstairs and visit with him and his latest lady, and she'd be all alone and . . .

She shut off the tap and looked up through the dwindling cloud of steam, expecting to find him still standing beside her, waiting for her response to his statement.

She was stunned to see him counting out four plates from a cupboard. He set three of them on the place mats already on the table.

"I need another one," he said. "At least, I think I do." He almost made it a question. "Isn't that why you cooked another package and made enough salad for a family of ten?"

Numbly, she opened a drawer and handed him a fourth woven-rattan rectangle, remembering the Mother's Day when he'd given her a set of a dozen. How the heck many children did he expect her to have? she'd wondered then, filled with anger and disappointment.

She'd had her eye on a hot-pink angora sweater trimmed with dainty flowers made from satin and beads.

Rand selected cutlery as if born to the task. She shook her head at the utter strangeness of the sight of him doing something so domestic. It was as if he were trying to prove something to her. Something so outrageous, she couldn't possibly believe it.

No matter what he said, Rand had not changed. Not that much. He was up to something, and whatever it was, she didn't think she liked it.

Did he mean to wriggle into the house again, then make her so miserable she'd leave? And leave the kids for him and his girlfriend? It wasn't going to work.

"Don't buck me on this, Rand," she said. "It's too important to let it become another bone of contention. The kids need two adults living in this house, and I plan to see that they have it, whether you approve or not."

"Of course," he said. "My approval to whatever course of action you chose was never very high on your list of requirements, was it?"

"When something is impossible to attain, a person quits trying," she said, and turned away, meaning to call the kids for dinner. "No one can live with constant disapproval."

"Kat." He caught her arm, pulling her back around to face him, locking one hand over her hair at the nape of her neck. "It was never so much disapproval as wanting . . . something else. I may not have liked what you did, but I always accepted your right to do what you had to do."

"Oh, Rand. You delude yourself about so much!"

"Do I?"

"Yes. If you accepted my right to have a job, to continue with my career, why did you go out of your way to make it almost impossible for me to do it? I could have succeeded at both my 'jobs' with your help and cooperation."

He swallowed. She watched his Adam's apple bob up and down in his throat. "Are you sure *you're* not deluding *yourself* about that?"

"Yes. I'm doing it now, Rand, as you may have noticed. I have my career. I'm taking care of my children and my home."

"But not your husband." His voice was soft.

So was hers. "I don't have a husband."

They stood there, staring at each other. Apart from their accidental touching when the pot boiled over, it was the closest they had been in a very long time. Kat's heart beat hard in her chest. Too hard. Too fast. Too erratic. Her throat ached. Her eyes burned.

Rand reached up and touched her throat with two gentle fingers, covering the wild pulse there. She drew in a sharp breath.

His hand trembled. He moved it to her waist, tightening his other around her nape. Seeing pain in her eyes, he loosened his grip. The pain remained. And . . . need?

A responsive need leaped in him. One minute it wasn't there, the next he was filled with a terrible kind of sexual urgency that scared the bejesus out of him. He understood in that moment how a man might simply take what he wanted.

Let her go, he ordered his hands. Step back, he ordered his legs. But as if held by an electromagnet, his body remained against hers, soaking up her heat.

Rand tried again to move away, but no one had ever aroused him as Kat could. He sucked in a harsh breath, wanting and yet not wanting this, willing it away, seeking control. But control slipped further and further out of reach with each spasmodic rise and fall of her breasts. He needed to feel her closer, needed more than this. He was going to do it. He had to do it. And he didn't much care what the outcome was.

He slid his hand from her nape down her back, over her taut buttocks, dragging her even tighter against him. "But this is no delusion, is it, Kat?" he muttered, pressing her to his hardness. He brought one hand up and cupped a full breast. The nipple jutted hard into his palm. "Nor is this."

A sound like a sob jerked out of her, and she squeezed her eyes shut. Her mouth twisted as if she were about to cry. He covered it with his own and felt her lips tremble apart, her tongue seek the taste of him.

Oh, Lord! She felt good against him, he thought giddily, moving her back and forth in an erotic little dance. She felt right. She tasted right. She smelled right. Baby powder. Perfume. Woman. His woman. She planted her palms on his chest, maybe meaning to shove him away. He raised his head, met her startled, distressed gaze, said her name again.

"Rand . . ." Her voice was high and thin. "Don't . . ." Her breath caught in her throat, and her eyes flooded with tears again. Her hands slid up around his shoulders, not pushing away but holding now, fingers touching the skin above his collar. "Oh, God, we can't— We shouldn't—"

"Babe . . ." He brushed his mouth over hers. Her lips parted. "We are. We must. We . . . Kat—" Her tongue came out, just the tip, beguiling him as she touched her top lip with it. With a soft, broken moan he kissed her again.

Ah, the taste of her! He could drown in it, lose himself, if he didn't stop now.

He cradled her head between his hands and looked down at her as he tilted her face up. Her eyes, shadowed by her lashes, held intense pain. The eggshell whiteness of her skin told him even more.

"I'm sorry," he whispered. "I'm so sorry about . . . everything."

She nodded jerkily, like a marionette whose strings were too tight. "Me, too, Rand, but it's too late for that. We blew it apart. We can never put it back together again."

He drew a deep breath. "Kat, do you want to?"

She searched his gaze for a long moment, then shook her head. "No, Rand."

He could see that she meant it. His heart ached like never before, and a few more pieces of it cracked and fell away. He lifted a lock of her hair and let it trickle through his fingers. "I'm such a fool. I guess I should go, huh?"

Her head bobbed up and down. "Better . . . that . . . way." He could see she was almost at the breaking point. He dropped the last few strands of her hair.

"Didja find any, Dad?"

Kat's eyes went wild and panicky as she snatched herself away from him, tearing her gaze from his face to the kids.

"Dinner's ready, go wash your hands," she said in a rush, flapping her hands at Nathan and Katie. "Go!"

"Find any what?" Rand asked.

"Any lice," Nathan said.

Rand backed up until the counter stopped him. Kat's face held guilt, horror, shame, a dozen other emotions he couldn't quite read. Jeeze! Lice? Poor Kat. She must have hated that.

"He wasn't looking for lice," Katie said. "He was gonna kiss her. Go ahead, Daddy, do it. You, too, Mom. Kiss and make up."

Kat made a small choked sound, and Rand turned to her, suddenly laughing because it beat the hell out of crying in front of his kids. If only it could be that easy!

"Sure," he said. "Why don't we, Kitty-Kat? Come on, let's kiss and make up."

She whirled away from him and bolted from the room. He heard the front door slam and took one step after her, but he tripped over Katie and had to catch the corner of the table to regain his balance.

The kids both stared at him, eyes wide. Katie was the first to speak. She looked disappointed. "Why did Mommy run away? Is she mad at me for asking you to kiss her?"

"No, honey." He looked at his children, wishing life were as simple as they thought it was. No, Kat was mad at him. Kat had been mad at him for a long time, and he should be used to it. "You heard your mother," he said, "go get washed while I dish up."

Where had Kat gone? When would she come back? And what the hell was he going to say when she did?

THREE

It was late when Kat returned home.

Rand was waiting, sitting in a pool of light in the living room. He'd leaned his head against the back of the upholstered chair. He didn't lift it when she came through the front door, only opened his eyes.

She stiffened. "You shouldn't put your head—"

"Don't worry," he said, his tone easy. But his eyes, she noticed, were watchful. "I'm sure it's fine. Did you vacuum?"

"Well, yes, several times, but I haven't shampooed the upholstery yet."

"Vacuuming's plenty, Kat. What you were doing today was . . . overkill."

She leaned wearily against the arch between the entry and the living room. She must have walked ten angry, confused miles that evening. "How would you know?"

He grinned again as he got to his feet. "Trust me,

I know. I've had 'em. You vacuum the furniture, wash the bedding, the clothing, the brushes and combs, and shampoo with the right soap, and you're fine. Until the next time."

He must have picked them up on one of his third-world assignments, she thought. She supposed she should be glad he'd gotten rid of them before coming home. She didn't want to think about how he'd caught them.

"There won't be a next time," she said resolutely.

"Maybe, maybe not. I had cooties at least twice while I was growing up."

Kat dropped down onto the arm of a chair. Her eyes widened, partly with relief because she'd kicked off her shoes, partly in disbelief. "You?"

"Yeah, sure." His perplexed frown looked so much like Katie's, it was all she could do not to laugh. "Why *not* me?"

"Because . . ." She shook her head and chewed on her lower lip. From all that Rand had told her about his mother, she was a paragon of maternal virtue. And she had let Rand get cooties? No! Of course not. The idea was ludicrous.

Kat had had them once herself, as a child, and would never forget the shame of it. As she had done, her mother had gone to a strange drugstore to buy the shampoo to cure the problem and had forbidden her to play ever again with the Sheltenham kids down the road. The Sheltenhams had just moved in, kept a goat in their backyard, three mostly wrecked pickup trucks in the weedy front yard, and had eight children. The kids played their music really loud, stayed up until they got tired, and lived by no rules or routine that Kat had ever discerned.

She'd thought they were the neatest family she'd ever met.

"Feel better after your walk?" Rand asked, pacing to the far side of the room. He picked up a vase, looked at its bottom as if checking for a price tag, then set it down again with great care.

"I'm all right," she said to his back. "Thank you for staying."

His tone was dry as he turned and said, "Not that you gave me many options."

"No. I don't suppose I did." She forced herself to go on meeting his gaze. "I hope you didn't have a date or . . . anything."

Rand thought about the fish fillet now likely fully thawed in his refrigerator. "Nothing that wouldn't keep." The disgusting orange glop that the kids had shoveled in so industriously hadn't tasted too bad, his enjoyment coming from eating it in their company, in the home he still thought of as his. The best relish, however, would have been Kat's presence too.

He crossed the room to stand before her. "Are you hungry?" he asked. "You didn't take time to eat before you . . . flew away."

"On my broomstick?" He heard the bitterness in her tone.

"I didn't say that, Kat. I didn't even mean to suggest it."

She pulled a face. "I know. Sorry. That was . . . bitchy."

She spoke reluctantly, he thought, as if unwilling to concede that maybe this time there hadn't been any

know you didn't mean anything by it. And you were right. I did need some time to myself. I get very little of that. With a nanny in residence, I hope to get a bit more."

His mouth twisted up on one side in what she thought he meant to be another smile. It had no effect on the bleakness in his eyes. "Funny," he said. "I get too much time to myself."

She changed the subject without commenting. "I want you to know that I do try to look after the kids properly, Rand," she said earnestly. "Please believe that. I don't neglect them because of the pressures of my job. I never let them go to bed dirty. I can't think where they got . . . cooties except at day care." Funny, but calling them "cooties" made them less of a threat to her sanity. "That's why they aren't going back."

"Kat . . ." He walked toward her again, his steps long and slow, like a large animal on the prowl. Hair stood up on the back of her neck, on her arms. Something in his eyes reminded her of when he'd dragged her against him in the kitchen and shown her what he was feeling. And put a name to her own feelings.

"The kids didn't get head lice because you let them go dirty," he said. His voice was a low rumble that made her goose bumps smooth out, working a kind of magic on her jangled nerves. His voice sounded as if he were holding her, soothing her, caring for her. "I know that. They got them because someone in their school, or maybe, as you think, in the day-care center, had them. Head lice get passed around like the common cold. There is no shame in it."

She clenched her teeth again. "I'm sure your *mother*

felt shame, even if you didn't. Assuming you weren't lying about having had them as a child simply to make me feel better. Rand, I know what a good mother she was. She was perfect. She—"

He cut her off by putting two fingers across her lips, briefly. The shock of his touch was enough to keep her from saying more about his mother, which was just as well. He had always refused to discuss his parents. Long ago, Kat had realized he found the subject of his being orphaned at sixteen too painful to recount beyond the bare fact that it had happened.

"You always did sweat the small stuff too much," he said. "Forget it, Kat. Where did you go, to the beach?"

She nodded, keeping her eyes on him, lest he move to touch her again. She must be prepared for it. For the electric jolt it sent through her body. She couldn't let him know how deeply he could still affect her.

"The tide was out," she said. "I walked along the shore for miles."

"I remember how you liked to walk and walk when stress got to you. I'm sorry if my showing up here today stressed you out."

"It wasn't so much your showing up as it was the . . . circumstances."

She wrapped her arms around herself. "Yucch! When I found out why the kids and I were so itchy, I nearly went mad. I felt *filthy*! I scrubbed all of us, did piles and piles of laundry, vacuumed everything in sight, but still I felt dirty. And I continued to itch."

Damn, but it felt good, just telling another adult what she'd been through. The kids didn't understand, of course, and there was no one else she'd even consider sharing this with. She was just glad Craig had been too busy for the past couple of weeks to go dancing, or she might have given them to him. And Todd—he hadn't been around for about a month, filling in for another pilot on the Toronto-Miami run.

Craig would not have been amused at getting cooties from his ballroom-dancing partner. Todd, on the other hand, might have been.

"Is that what today was all about?" Rand asked, his smile sympathetic. "Because you continued to itch?"

"No." She squeezed her eyes shut for a second. "Today was because I continued to itch for a damn good reason." She met his gaze reluctantly. "*I* was reinfested. I don't think the kids were, but I shampooed myself again—and them, just in case—and started all over on the house. Only this time, I meant to do it better."

His eyes danced, and she thought he'd laugh. Oddly, now that she had faced his knowing, she realized that his laughter wouldn't have been as shattering as she'd thought. She almost wished he would laugh. It was a sound she'd once very much liked to hear ringing through their house, especially when it had echoed in the mostly unfurnished and entirely uncarpeted cavities the rooms had been those first few years.

"I can't think how it happened a second time," she went on quickly to purge her mind of foolish thoughts. "I must have missed one." She smiled. "A pregnant one."

He chuckled. "This time, I'm sure you didn't. The way you were scrubbing things, you can't have missed a nit."

"Lordy, I hope not."

His smile caught a small corner of her heart, tugging at it. She knew she should say something, preferably something witty, but suddenly there seemed to be nothing more to say. All she could do was look at him and wonder what he was thinking. Probably, she mused, he was trying to come up with a graceful way of making his exit.

He must be as embarrassed as she was by what had happened to them in the kitchen. Would she ever forget the note of horror in his voice when he'd said, "Kat . . . do you want to?" What would he have done if she'd said yes?

She choked back a semihysterical laugh. If she hadn't run out of the house, then he would have. She'd seen the regret painted all over his features when he'd said, "I'm such a fool."

She felt like a fool for the way she'd responded to him, and she wished *she* knew a graceful way to release him from what he probably saw as an obligation to stay a bit longer.

She still had to do her own room before she could go to bed—scrub it, not merely vacuum, regardless of what the shampoo bottle and Rand said about it. She was more than merely tired now. Her legs shook with exhaustion. Her hands trembled so badly, she had to stuff them into the pockets of her jeans. Deciding that graceful didn't matter anymore, she opened her mouth to tell him to go. "Would you . . . would you like some coffee?"

Oh, that was stupid! That was no way out of this awkward situation.

He glanced at his watch, as if to see if he had the time. Her throat tightened, and she was about to withdraw her invitation when he said, "Sure. I made a pot after supper. Most of it's still left." Slipping an arm around her shoulders, he turned her to a chair. "You sit. I'll get it."

This, from the man who, two years before, could scarcely pour himself a glass of water from a jug in the fridge? She collapsed into the chair, closed her eyes, and leaned her head back. Maybe vacuuming was adequate after all.

"I think you'd be better off without this," Rand said when he returned. Startled, Kat opened her eyes and sat upright. She'd been about to fall asleep, listening to him clatter things in the kitchen.

He carried a round metal tray with two steaming mugs of coffee and a plate of date loaf. He must have taken the bread from the freezer right after dinner; it appeared fully thawed, and he'd buttered the thick slices. Rand had always liked the desserts she seldom had the time or energy to make. Or much interest in. Inanely, she was glad she'd picked up several sweet loaves at a local discount store last month and frozen them.

"You look as if you need sleep more than anything," he continued, handing her the coffee.

"I'll be all right."

"Well, drink up, so you can get to bed. It's all ready for you to slide into."

She stared at him through the steam of her coffee. "My *bed*? But—"

"Don't worry. I vacuumed it first." He grinned. "And I didn't miss a nit, either."

She subsided back against the cushions. "I . . . you didn't have to do that for me, Rand." She bit into a slice of the date loaf. Not surprisingly, since she'd missed dinner, she was hungry. In seconds she'd demolished it.

"I wanted to do it for you," he said. "I had nothing much to do once the kids were in bed and the dishes done."

She closed her eyes, trying to visualize Rand loading a dishwasher, Rand stretching a fitted sheet over a mattress. . . . Either picture defied imagination.

"See what a good nanny I'd make?" he said.

She opened her eyes, lifted her mug, and sipped. He leaned forward, arms on his thighs. "Kat, let's just try it. Let's see if it'll work."

"Rand, stop it. Please. You know it wouldn't work. And it would hurt the kids so badly. You heard Katie— you saw the looks on both their faces.

"Like all children of divorced parents, they desperately want to believe there's a chance of our getting back together again. It's a fantasy they'll likely live with until one of us dies. We can't do anything that might reinforce that fantasy, give it any kind of substance for them to build on."

She set her cup down carefully, keeping her gaze pinned on him as she added, "Because we are not, ever, going to get back together again, Rand."

He gazed right back at her, long and levelly. "Aren't we, Kat?"

"No!" Her reply was as swift as it was explosive, and she shot out of her chair.

"You seem very sure of that, Kat, but when we—"

"If you're talking about that little incident in the kitchen, Rand, I did a lot of thinking while I was walking. It was a momentary aberration, nothing more.

We'd been remembering Jenny and Karl. Our emotions were running high. Death—thinking about it—often makes people instinctively try to reassure themselves that they are alive."

He smiled wryly. "Well, we're both reassured on that count, aren't we?"

"Not that you required it, I'm sure."

He rose, moving in close. Nearly a head taller than she, he forced her to look up at him. "And you did?"

She clenched her fists at her sides. "If that's a not-too-subtle way of asking about my sex life, I remind you that it's none of your business. So long as I'm discreet and keep that side of my affairs apart from the children, you have no call to comment."

"Affairs?" he fired back at her. "In the plural? I'm surprised you have time, what with the children, the house, your career, and all the little extra . . . nit-picking chores you have to do. You certainly never had much time for me."

She flung her head back. "Not that you let that interfere with *your* sex life."

For a long moment they faced each other, bitter adversaries again.

Kat spoke first, through her teeth. "I repeat, if you moved into the suite, the children's hopes would be built up cruelly, uselessly. We both know how futile it would be for the two of us to try getting along for more than fifteen minutes at a time. Didn't we just prove that?"

"The kids wouldn't be hurt if we made it clear from the beginning that I was moving in solely to give them the best care possible while you're at work."

She laughed, and the sound of it hurt him. Her eyes

were cold. She was right. They couldn't get along for more than fifteen minutes. He wanted music and sun dance. She gave him discord and ice—and the back of her head as she walked away to pick up something one of the kids had left lying around. A small figure with a round head and a cylindrical body. It looked as wooden as he felt. He slumped back down into his chair.

"I'd still need someone to take them to school and pick Katie up," she said. "Kindergarten's out at eleven-forty-five. Nathan's finished school at three. They both need to be met. Those hours wouldn't, I'm sure, fit in well with your schedule, even if you're not taking out-of-town assignments anymore." She gave him a pained glance. "Not many employers let staff leave their desks to run and fetch kids from school."

"I haven't had a desk at the paper for almost as long as I've been staying in town. This being the electronic age, I've been working at home." He picked up the previous day's newspaper, which he'd been scanning while she was out. Folding it open to the editorial pages, he showed her his weekly cartoon.

She walked closer, and he watched her brows knit as if she still didn't understand what he was getting at. "*This* is what I do now, Kat," he explained, tapping the page. "Every Wednesday. In addition to a column and whatever freelance work I can pick up."

That cartoon? Kat thought. That was his work? She stared at it and gnawed on her bottom lip, filled with dismay as understanding finally dawned.

It could mean only one thing. He was broke. He was broke because he'd relinquished his lucrative position as senior reporter in foreign affairs so he'd be available for his visitation weekends. He must have—

they must have—been draining his savings steadily over the past two years.

This was why he wanted to move into the basement suite!

"Oh, Rand!" she said, lifting her gaze to him. He was making do with what he could earn cartooning and freelancing? The thought appalled her. He'd always taken such pride in his ability to provide for his family. That, of course, had been one of the biggest hurdles to trip them up. He'd wanted to do it all on his own, and she'd had just as great a need to be financially independent.

But cartooning? Freelancing? For a man who'd once held one of the highest-paying jobs with the *Mainlander*, British Columbia's largest evening paper, it had to be a precarious existence.

Guilt gnawed at her. All the while she'd sat back comfortably, earning an excellent salary, still taking what he paid toward the children's support, blithely accepting his share of the mortgage payments and never guessing how pressed he must be.

Naturally, she'd known that he loved his children. She hadn't realized, though, what he'd been willing to sacrifice for them. No more volcanoes. No more earthquakes. No more race riots and violent third-world elections. And no more hefty paychecks and huge bonuses.

"Just freelancing?" she whispered. "And a cartoon once a week?"

She remembered his first cartoons. Two hundred dollars apiece. Even if the price had gone up, say to two-fifty, at one a week, they'd bring him in only a thousand dollars a month. Exactly what he paid toward the children's support. His half of the mortgage payment must come out of his freelance earnings. That and his own rent and other expenses. How could he possibly afford all of it?

The fact was, he couldn't. And what he was trying to tell her without coming right out and saying so, was that he needed her help. The thought of Rand, such a proud, stubborn man, reduced to begging his ex-wife for a room to sleep in, dropped her back down into her chair.

"Rand!" she said again. "Oh, Lord, I'm so sorry. I had no idea. You see, I haven't been taking the paper because I never have time to read it, so I never noticed that your byline was missing and . . . I only bought that one to check on my ad. I feel like such a . . ."

She worried at her lower lip with her teeth. "I can— the kids and I can make do with much less, of course! It wouldn't hurt any of us. You've always been more than generous and . . . well, I've had a couple of promotions since the divorce."

Clutching the arms of her chair, she leaned forward. "Why didn't you tell me you were in financial difficulties? I feel as if we've made you destitute."

He stared at her, a dull red flush climbing up his face, and she wished she'd been more tactful. She should never have blurted out that she understood. She should have found some way to save his pride— at the very least.

"Kat! Wait a minute," he said. "You've got the wrong idea altogether. I'm not destitute. I'm—"

Cutting him off with a wave of her hand, she jumped to her feet again. "Of course you're not. I don't for one minute think you are. That was just a figure of speech.

But I can understand that you may be feeling a bit of a pinch."

She shouldn't have used that word, "destitute." It was a degrading term. No wonder he was so quick to deny it. She might just as well have called him a "welfare bum."

"But if—if it'll help," she went on, "of course you can have the suite. You can move in whenever you want. Tomorrow, if you like."

"I can?" His jaw dropped. He closed his mouth, then asked, as if he needed it clarified, "I can move into the suite?"

Kat pulled herself together and nodded. She'd said it. Despite Rand's stunned appearance, she knew he'd heard her perfectly. She couldn't very well rescind the offer now.

"Tomorrow?" he asked.

"Yes."

He blinked, then smiled, a slowly growing smile that finally covered his entire face. It curved his mouth, creased his cheeks, and fanned into the crow's-feet at the corners of his eyes. Even his ears looked glad. His entire expression seemed vaguely familiar, but she couldn't recall when *she'd* made him that happy before. Usually, all she'd done was disappoint him.

Not this time, though. She wondered dimly at his obvious joy over her agreement, his almost palpable relief. There was more to this than his simply wanting to be near the kids.

Of course, she thought. It was the beginning of the month. His rent was likely due. Maybe he didn't even have it this month!

She strode across the room and adjusted the vertical blinds, which didn't need adjusting. Turning, she caught him staring at her as if he still couldn't believe she'd meant it. "That is," she added, "we can try it for . . . for a few months."

In a few months maybe his freelance work would pick up. In a few months maybe she'd be able to convince him that the kids didn't need as much support money as he insisted on giving them. In a few months summer vacation would be over, and Katie, like Nathan, would be in school virtually all day. The need for child care, while not obviated entirely, would be greatly reduced.

In a few months maybe she'd remember just how bad their marriage had finally become, and all these churning, nebulous emotions that had prompted her insane invitation would release their grip on her.

"If it doesn't work out," she said briskly when his gaze threatened to ignite her, "we'll have to reassess, naturally. But for the time being, well, of course you can move in."

She bit her lip again. She was determined to show him that this was nothing more than a sensible solution to two separate problems, one hers, the other his. "I had no idea you'd given up so much in order to stay in town to be near the kids. I . . . I'm grateful to you for making that sacrifice—for their sakes—and I'm willing to help, especially since it will help me too."

He rose and came to stand before her. She thought for a minute he would touch her. Her skin tingled. He didn't touch her. Her skin continued to tingle.

"Thank you, Kat." His voice was that low, soft rumble that smoothed out all her rough edges. "I don't know what else to say, except . . . thank you. This means a lot to me. My place isn't big. My drawing board in one end of the living room sort of cramps things, as does my computer setup in my bedroom. I had to keep the second bedroom free for the kids' visits, but here, I won't have to do that, will I?"

He beamed happily again. "It'll be great having a room just for work. That way I won't be tripping over power hookups and the fax machine and all the rest of it all the time.

"This will work," he went on, eagerly, and this time he took her hands in his. "You'll see. It'll be perfect for me, for all of us. Them, because they'll have both of us. You, because you won't have to be concerned about them at all, and me, because I'll get to see them every day. I'll have plenty of time to work, too, when they're in school."

He rubbed his thumbs over her knuckles, the side of one catching the stones of her diamond ring, turning it back and forth. The friction of the smooth metal against her skin ignited a band of fire around her finger that somehow transferred itself to her chest.

She snatched her hands away and tucked them behind her back. Their gazes remained locked; then she quickly turned away because it was too hard to go on looking at Rand. She straightened the paper he'd thrown untidily on an end table.

"When do you intend to move in?" she asked.

Behind her, he said, "Would tomorrow be too soon?"

She shook her head and shoved her hands into her pockets as she faced him again. "No. Of course not. I already said you could." It would be too soon.

The thought crossed her mind that it would also be too late.

Everything was much too late. Stiffly, she walked over to a wall unit and opened a drawer. From it, she took a key to the back door, one for the door to the suite, and, after a moment's hesitation, another for the front. She dropped them into his hand.

"Thanks," he whispered. He looked at her for a long time, and she thought he might say something more, but all he said was a quiet "Good night, Kat."

She forced herself to look directly into his eyes. "Good night, Rand."

For a moment his head dipped as if he might kiss her. She wanted to back away, but something kept her rooted in place. She steeled herself, tightening her body to withstand the shock she knew his lips would bring, to prevent the trembling she could feel beginning deep within.

With a quick shake of his head he stepped back. He lifted one hand in a half-wave and slipped out. Oddly, he left her with the impression that he was as relieved as she that he hadn't kissed her.

When her heart had quit pounding almost explosively hard, she locked the door behind him. She took the tray to the kitchen, frowning at the half-full cups of cold coffee, the mostly uneaten date bread on the plate. She ate another slice, wrapped and refrigerated the rest, then turned off all the lights and went to her room.

It wasn't until she was almost asleep that she remembered the time she'd seen that look of utter joy on Rand's face before.

It was when she'd said she'd marry him.

Too bad the marriage had outlived the ecstasy. But that was life.

FOUR

Nathan stared at Kat in disbelief. "Daddy's going to live here?"

"Not here . . . *here*," Kat stressed, waving an arm to indicate the main floor of the house. "In the basement suite. The only time he'll be up here is when I'm not at home."

Nathan leaned forward, his elbows on the breakfast table, his chin on his hands, a sly smile on his face. "You're really going to get married again, huh?" His dark eyes shone. "Pretty soon, I mean. You're just not telling us yet. You want to surprise us or something."

Kat groaned inwardly. This was going to be a lot harder than she'd anticipated. "No, sweetheart. We're not going to get married again. Not pretty soon. Not ever. We are two separate people with two separate lives, exactly as we've been since our divorce. I want both of you to understand that."

She could see both Nathan and Katie struggling with a concept too big for their meager experience to take in. They and Mommy and Daddy would live in the same house, but they weren't going to be a family again? Incomprehensible.

Haltingly, trying to go slowly so they'd understand as fully as possible, Kat spent the next half hour attempting to explain what still seemed almost inexplicable to her. How could she expect a couple of little children to grasp her foolish, impulsive behavior?

"So you see," she said in conclusion, "it doesn't mean that we are going to be living together as a family again. Daddy and I still don't get along the way a married couple should. We don't love each other that way. But we are going to be friends again, and as always, we both love the two of you very much."

"We can see Dad every day, right? And you too?" Nathan asked. Kat nodded. "Good!" He jumped up and hugged her, burrowing close. "It's gonna be great! Now we can all spend the weekends together, and we won't have to be lonely for either of you. Right, Mom?"

"Damn," Kat said softly, lowering her head into the palm of one hand.

Weekends! That was one complication she hadn't considered. Would Rand still insist on his weekends with the kids, though he'd be seeing them daily now? And if he did, what was she supposed to do? He didn't have room in the basement suite for them to sleep down there, not if he was going to set up his drawing board and computer in the second bedroom. It would mean him coming up here to be with them.

And with her.

That simply would not do.

"No," she said firmly, facing the children. "We

won't be spending the weekends together. When it's your dad's weekend with you, I'll—I'll go away somewhere."

Katie's face fell. "No, Mommy! I don't want you to go away. I want you to stay with us. Where are you going to go?"

Relief swept over Kat. Was this her way out? Yes! It would be much too hard on the kids, Katie in particular, to cope with this. Her first instinct had been right. It wasn't going to work.

"Nowhere, baby," she said quickly, scooping her daughter onto her lap. "Not if you don't want me to."

"I don't. I like you to tuck me in. And I like Daddy to tuck me in too." She smiled up at Kat. "Now, you can both do it together, right, Mom?"

Kat hesitated, then shook her head. "No, I don't think so, hon. Remember what I said about separate lives. Daddy will have his own schedule, especially when I'm here. We won't want to interfere with that."

"Sure we will," said Rand.

Kat jumped, twisting around in her chair. He was standing right behind her. She watched him bend to kiss Katie, then Nathan, his head very close to hers. Then, before she could react in any way, he turned and planted a quick, hard kiss on her lips, eyes dancing playfully.

For a long moment their gazes clashed, and his laughter faded. His dark eyes probed hers as if seeking something specific. She didn't know if he found it, but he looked away first, saying to Katie, "My schedule will normally permit me to tuck you in, angel face, if that's what you want."

Katie flung herself off Kat's lap into her father's arms, while Nathan tugged at his wrist, demanding that he follow and see something important in his bedroom.

As her children dragged their father away, Kat shoved her chair back and stacked their three cereal bowls in the sink. She ran water over them, letting it cool her wrists as she did so.

Rand and the kids crossed behind her, heading downstairs to the suite.

She turned off the water, listening. Her throat tightened as she heard him come back up, but he didn't open the door that led from the landing into the laundry room, and thence the kitchen. She heard a car door slam, footsteps again, the kids excitedly demanding to be allowed to help him unpack.

After carefully drying her hands, she slipped into the powder room and tidied her hair, smoothed fingertips over her eyebrows, then over the pale lips Rand had so recently kissed. She looked at the eyes his searching gaze had plumbed. Their gray color resembled dirty laundry water. Her lashes, while thick and long, were too pale to be interesting. She found herself wishing she'd put on mascara that morning, a bit of lipstick. Had her mouth tasted of cereal and milk?

Oh, hell! She slammed her palms onto the counter and squeezed her eyes shut. What was the matter with her? She must have been crazy last night.

In her mind's eye she saw his hand, brown, large, with thin tufts of black hair on the backs of his fingers, closing over the three keys. It had felt almost as if that hand were closing gently around her heart, her very life, capturing it again.

No! She shook her head. She hadn't been readmitting him into her life. She'd simply been giving him the keys to a house he had as much right to live in as she did. They could and would keep their private lives separate. Despite their children.

Feeling overheated and disturbed, she stomped back into the kitchen, snatched up her shoulder bag, and wrenched open the door to the basement. "Hurry up, you two!" she called down the stairs. "Let's get a move on or you'll be late for school."

"Do you want me to take them?" Rand poked his head around the door of the suite.

She glared at him, feeling that her every fractured emotion was all his fault.

"No," she said curtly, and earned herself a questioning look from her son.

"You didn't sound very friendly when Daddy said good-bye," he accused her as they walked down the sunny sidewalk on the way to school. "You said you were going to be friends again."

"I know, and we will be. The same kind of casual friends that Mrs. Gold and I were. We'll talk when we see each other. We'll compare notes about our workdays, about the weather." She smiled. "And, of course, about you guys. But I'll still have my other friends, and your dad will have his."

"Girlfriends?"

"Of course."

"What if we don't like them?" Katie asked.

"I'm sure you will, but in any case, I'll expect you to remember to be very polite."

"Like I have to be to Craig," Nathan said with disgust. He disliked Craig, though he thought Todd was "excellent." "What if it hurts Dad's feelings when you have your friends over?"

"It won't. And," she added quickly to forestall the next logical question, "it won't hurt my feelings when he has his friends over."

After leaving the children at the door of their school, Kat hurried home, slipping into her car without going inside the house. She'd take care of some errands, then check in at the office and tell them her life was getting back to normal, that she'd return to work the next morning.

Back to normal, she thought as she hit the main arterial road across White Rock. Would things ever be "normal" again?

"Mommy says you and her aren't going to love each other again," Katie said to Rand, "and that it won't hurt her feelings when you have ladies over to visit. Is it going to hurt yours when Craig and Todd come to see her?"

Rand had heard tidbits about Craig and Todd for more than a year. He still hadn't learned to like it. He finished hanging a picture, then answered his daughter while he stood back to look at his work. "Only if they show up at the same time and have a big fight over her or something."

She giggled. "That's silly. Grown-ups don't fight."

Oh, yes, they do, Rand wanted to say. Grown-ups do fight. Terribly. Catastrophically. Yet, in retrospect, he'd preferred those fights to the icy quiet that had stolen over their home in the last months before they'd separated.

"You look sad, Daddy."

He forced himself to smile at her. "How could I be sad when I have you for a daughter?"

"I don't know," she said. Then, as if she didn't believe his denial, she patted his hand. "It'll be okay, Daddy."

"Will it, love?"

She nodded solemnly. "Know what always makes me feel better, Daddy?"

He crouched beside her and looped his arms around her. "What, Katie?"

"Cookies."

"Really. I suppose that means you'd like one."

She nodded earnestly.

He laughed and stood. "I think we have time for a cookie before we go pick up Nathan."

"Mommy always gives me twenty."

He picked her up, draping her over his shoulder, and strode out of his bedroom and into the galley-sized kitchen, where he seriously doubted he'd find so much as one cookie. Maybe she'd settle for cheese and crackers.

"You, my little love," he said, "are a con artist of the first water."

He set her down on a chair by the small table.

"What's a con artist?"

"That's what we call a little girl who tries to get what she wants by not telling the truth."

She looked so guilty, he had to relent. As he spread cheese from a jar onto a cracker, he added, "I'm sure your mother has told you how bad lying is."

He knew how Kat felt about lying. Her father had lied to her mother for years. She hated liars.

He frowned. Was letting her believe that he had to live in the basement suite because he couldn't afford his apartment really a lie? He liked to think not. He'd have told her the truth if she hadn't jumped to the wrong conclusion.

He'd been poised to do so, all set to give her a dozen and one reasons why it would be best if she agreed to his moving into the suite and caring for the kids, when she'd suddenly said, "You can move in whenever you want."

Hell, he was human. He'd jumped at it. And he hadn't told Kat the truth.

But he hadn't actually lied, had he?

The question was, how would Kat see it when she found out?

"Oh. Hi." Kat stopped halfway through the kitchen door. She hadn't expected Rand to be in her kitchen. Nor had she expected him to be up to his elbows in cookie dough, with the kids flanking him, kneeling on stools, pressing out clown shapes with plastic cutters. Another thing she hadn't expected was the way her heart leaped inside her chest. This was ridiculous. She simply had to get a grip.

She set her purse on the table, balanced her brief-case on the seat of a chair, and rattled her car keys in her jacket pocket.

"Hi." A smile lurked in Rand's eyes as he turned and looked at her. "Sorry about the mess. I'll clean it up. We tried this downstairs, but there isn't room for three in my kitchen."

"That's okay." She let her keys go still. Their

jangling jangled her nerves. Katie ran over and wrapped floury arms around her. Kat crouched and hugged her daughter tightly. "How was school, Nate? What did you do?"

"Okay," he said as Katie ran back and climbed up on her stool again. "I got a star in reading. Todd called from Honolulu just after we got home." Nathan was proud of having a friend who called from different parts of the globe. He kept track of Todd's journeys on a world map the pilot had given him. "Dad said it was okay for me to answer before the machine got it, since he was here."

"Yes." Her gaze flew to Rand. His back was to her as he continued to work over the cookies. "Of course. It was fine."

Kat was just glad Rand hadn't answered her phone himself. She wondered if he'd had his hooked up yet. She wondered also if he'd given her number to his . . . friends, so they could call in the meantime. She sincerely hoped not. She'd be damned if she'd go running downstairs with messages for him from women whose names ended in *i*. Bambi. Trixi. *Cooti*. She grinned to herself, feeling justifiably nasty.

"Todd will be in town tomorrow," Nathan went on. "He said he'd take us on a tour of a 747 if we can be ready by nine o'clock. Can we, Mom? He said he'd even show me the cargo holds."

Kat glanced at Rand again. He was rolling out cookie dough with great care and concentration, the same kind of care and concentration she'd always noticed when he was drawing. She doubted if he'd even heard Nathan, let alone had his "feelings hurt" by Todd's message.

"I guess so, Nate," she said.

Katie wrinkled her nose. "I don't want to go, Mommy. Can I stay with you, Daddy, instead? Can I, please?"

"Katie, we discussed that before, remember?" Kat said quickly. "Your dad and I haven't talked about weekends, and, anyway, this one isn't his. It's not fair for us to interfere with his plans."

"But, Mommy . . ."

"Katie, the answer is no."

"Katherine . . ." Rand wrenched himself around and set the rolling pin down with such force, a dusting of flour puffed up around him, making it look as if smoke were pouring out of him. "I'm perfectly capable of answering for myself, and since Katie asked me, not you, I think you should let me decide. I have no plans for tomorrow in the daytime, so Katie can stay with me."

She didn't miss his faint stress on the time of day. Meaning he *did* have plans for tomorrow night? Dammit, what could she say without sounding like a monster who was forcing her daughter to do something she didn't want to do when there was a perfectly viable alternative?

She wasn't too keen herself on crawling around the bowels of a 747, but since Nathan would enjoy it, she'd go along. The thought crossed her mind that maybe she should stay home with Katie and send Rand with Todd and Nathan. The inner workings of any conveyance were usually of far more interest to males than females.

It almost made her smile, thinking of the look on Rand's face if she suggested it.

"All right, then," she said.

Rand's smile was one of pure satisfaction. "I'll be free until around eight in the evening," he said, "so Katie's welcome to spend the entire day with me if she wants. You'll be spending the evening at home, I assume, this being your weekend with the kids?"

Apparently, he had no intention of giving up the alternate weekend plan. Of course not. He likely went on little weekend getaways whenever he could. The first time they'd made love had been on one of those. There was no reason to assume his seduction patterns had changed. She bit the inside of her cheek so hard, she tasted blood. *She* hadn't had a weekend getaway in longer than she could remember.

It was as if he were trying to point up the fact that he was free to have a date on Saturday night, but she was not. Dammit, she should have stuck to her guns and hired a nanny, not let her ex-husband back into her home. If he were a real nanny, he'd have to stay in, wouldn't he, if his employer wanted to go out?

She gripped her briefcase, slung her purse over her shoulder, and spun on one heel, leaving them to their cookie making.

In her room she tugged off her red linen blazer, flung it over a chair, slipped out of her navy skirt, and sent it after the blazer. Flopping down on her bed, she flung her hands over her head and gripped the brass spindles.

She wasn't being fair. If she'd hired a nanny, she'd still have had to negotiate time off for the woman. She wouldn't have been able to expect twenty-four-hour-a-day devotion, seven days a week. And there was nothing to say that she couldn't hire a baby-sitter if Todd wanted to do something purely adult for the evening.

Or that she couldn't simply feed the kids early and get them off to bed, then have Todd to the house for an intimate dinner for two.

A slow smile crossed her face as she gave that idea more thought. Yes, that was exactly what she'd do. And then, if Rand brought his date to show her his new apartment, she wouldn't have to sit there trying not to hear their voices and laughter rising into her part of the house.

Mrs. Gold had been a very quiet lady who seldom entertained. She couldn't expect the same consideration from Rand. And since she couldn't, why should he expect anything of the like from her?

Maybe she and Todd would be *very* noisy Saturday night.

However, it was still Friday night when Kat jumped at the sound of a knock on a door. Not an outer door, she realized when it came again, but an inner door. The one leading from the laundry room to the kitchen.

Rand! What could he want at—she glanced at her watch—quarter past ten in the evening? Why didn't he have a date? It crossed her mind that maybe he did. Maybe he'd brought the woman to meet her!

"Cooti, Cooti," she muttered to herself as she leaped to her feet. Somehow, though, it didn't bring a gleeful smile to her face. She whirled out of her office, ran down the four stairs from the bedroom level, along the hall and across the kitchen, then stopped just before opening the door. She glanced down at her thin cotton housecoat, which was all she wore. Should she rush up to her room for something more substantial?

Of course not! It was only Rand. He'd seen her in a lot less than this, and anyway, she was decently covered from neck to knees. Assuring herself there was no harm in him seeing her like this, she jerked open the door just as Rand raised his hand again.

At the sight of him, all alone, shirtless, his jeans hugging his hips low and tight, an ink stain on one cheek, her nipples popped right up to attention. As if they had bells attached, Rand's gaze dropped from her eyes to her chest. He stared.

She wanted to slam the door in his face, but he gripped its edge in one tight fist. She wanted to step back, but her bare feet seemed glued to the cool ceramic tiles of the floor.

"Hello," she said, amazed at how unruffled her voice sounded, despite her inner turmoil. She was determined not to let him know how sexually appealing she still found him. "Something I can do for you?"

Oh, Lord! Rand's mouth went dry at the sight of her. She could do things for him, all right! She *did* do things for him. And to him. She was only half-dressed! Her breasts were clearly outlined inside the thing she wore. She had, he was certain, nothing on under it. It had little buttons all the way down the front, from its plain neckline to its straight hem just at knee level. It was white cloth printed with little pink and blue flowers, gathered a bit to provide fullness over her breasts. It didn't provide nearly enough and was so entirely feminine, so immensely sexy, he wanted to rip it off her.

He wanted that almost as badly as he wanted to undo each one of those little buttons and remove the garment from her one tantalizing inch at a time.

He jerked his gaze from her breasts to her face

again, finding her expression bland, her smile small and conventional, but her eyes wary. Her cheeks were pink, her lips parted. Her chin, he saw, had a tremor so faint, he couldn't be completely sure it wasn't his imagination. He swallowed hard, trying to find enough saliva to wet his throat.

"Mind if I come in and use the phone?" he managed to say.

She shook her head, her hair all loose and swirly on her shoulders, drawing his gaze to its curly ends—and to her breasts again. He stared once more, still clinging to the door. His knees went weak.

"The phone?" she said. "You wanted to use it?"

"I—uh—yes. I'm sorry." He blinked and tore his gaze off her pertly erect nipples. "You . . . were, um, ready for bed. I shouldn't have disturbed you." Oh, hell! He wanted to disturb her, all right. He wanted her as disturbed as he was. Those sweet nipples of hers told him she was already close to that state. What would it take to drag her right to the brink with him? One kiss? Two? The flick of a thumbnail over a nipple? The stroke of a hand up over her bottom? A whisper of breath across her thighs? . . .

"Go ahead," she said, startling him. "Help yourself." He swayed and felt his jaw drop.

"Help . . . myself?"

She waved her hand toward the back wall of the kitchen. "Yes, of course. The phone's right over there where it always was."

"Oh. Yeah. The phone." He stared into her eyes for several seconds more. "Uh, you're . . . in the way," he said helplessly. If he touched her, if he so much as brushed against her while entering the kitchen, he knew it would be game over. He'd wrap her in his arms, devour her, smother her, overwhelm her. . . .

Kat felt a hot flush slide up her chest and over her face. What an idiot! Quickly, she stepped back. "Sorry. I . . . wasn't thinking." Of course she hadn't been thinking. She'd been standing there staring at his bare chest and shoulders, at all that expanse of brown male skin, the light dusting of hair down the center. She'd been mesmerized, stunned into near catatonia by a physique she'd seen thousands of times before.

As had too many other women as well, she reminded herself. They'd probably all gone into shock just as she did. That's what made it so easy for Rand.

"Excuse me," she said as he sidled past her, his gaze never leaving her face. "I have work to do." She spun around, nearly ran from the kitchen to her office, and slumped into her high-backed swivel chair. Pulling it up close to her desk, she hid there, head in her hands, hearing the murmur of his voice as he spoke on the phone.

She stared at the computer printouts between her elbows, none of the words or numbers registering on her brain. All she could think of was the thinness of her cotton robe and the way her nipples had stood at attention as she opened the door to Rand.

She knew he'd seen them. What had he thought? His face had told her nothing. How long had she gone on holding herself rigid so she wouldn't reach out and touch his chest? How long had she gaped at him?

Oh, Lordy! "You're in my way. . . . " She felt like more of a fool than she'd felt in a long time. *He'd had to tell her to get out of his way!* She'd stood there like an utter ninny and blocked the doorway while she ogled him!

A sound behind her sent her spinning around in her chair, gripping its arms tightly.

It was him, of course, looking oddly tentative, holding a chocolate-chip cookie in one hand. Once again her gaze was drawn to his bare chest. She blinked and forced herself to meet his eyes.

"Thank you," he said. "I had to call the paper with a couple of corrections before they went to print. It was important, or I wouldn't have bothered you. The phone company said they'd get me all hooked up tomorrow afternoon."

She folded her arms protectively across her breasts. "That's all right. It was no bother. I wasn't going to bed. I was working."

He nodded. "I see that." He looked around. "The spare room makes a good office for you."

She nodded. "Putting the brass bed in my room made space for a sofa bed in here, so I can still use this room for guests if I ever need to."

She'd willingly let him have their marriage bed with its super-firm mattress. He needed it for his bad back. Her brass bed was about the only major thing she'd brought into the marriage anyway. That and a fetus, of course.

He leaned in the doorway and munched his cookie. She supposed, since he'd baked it, he was entitled. "Do you have many overnight guests?" he asked. "I mean, who'd sleep in here?"

"No." No one had ever used the secondhand sofa bed. Like Rand, Kat had no family. That was one of the things that had drawn them together in the first place. They'd both longed for some kind of solid connection.

"I saw you had an almost-full pot of coffee in the kitchen," he went on. "Do you still drink it by the gallon, day and night?" He, and Jenny, had been appalled when she would drink two or three cups of coffee along with the babies' two o'clock feedings and still manage to sleep like the dead. It never seemed to bother the babies, either.

"Yes," she said. "It's what keeps me going, like fuel for a car."

"Could I bring you a cup—before I go back downstairs and let you get to work?"

Kat bit her lower lip. What was he up to? Why was he doing things like this, making cookies with the kids, offering to cater to her? What did he think it would prove? Whatever his aim, she knew it wouldn't last. He'd get tired of it sooner or later. Likely sooner.

Maybe she could help things along, simply so that the kids wouldn't get too used to it. Make him feel used, make him feel she was taking advantage of the good nature he was suddenly exhibiting. That should work, and quickly.

Accordingly, she took him up on the offer.

"Thank you," she said. "That would be nice."

Not at all to her surprise, he returned in minutes with a tray bearing two cups of coffee and a plate of cookies. He'd taken the time to pull on a T-shirt, though she wasn't sure it was much of an improvement. Still, when he asked if he could join her, she shrugged in silent assent.

If, as she'd told Katie and Nathan, she and Rand were going to be friends again, she'd have to make an effort to get along with him, to have the occasional conversation. She told herself that the more often she saw him at close quarters, the easier it would become to look at him and not salivate. That T-shirt really helped only minimally.

Besides, she had another, even more pressing need to talk to him, she thought, remembering the way he'd kissed her that morning along with the kids. He had to understand that he couldn't do it again.

That was just one more thing she didn't want the kids to get used to.

FIVE

To give herself a moment, Kat picked up a cookie and bit into it. Now that she had the opportunity, it was harder than she'd expected it to be, bringing up the matter of that little peck on the lips.

"Very good," she said of his cookies.

"Thank you." Still standing, he lifted a coffee mug and sipped. "You still make great coffee."

She nodded in acknowledgment of the compliment, at a complete loss for words.

"This is nice," he continued when the silence had gone on too long. "It's good of you to let me join you."

"I . . . was in need of a break. I suppose you were, too, since you've been working all evening as well."

"I'm used to working evenings," he said, lowering himself to the plaid sofa and leaning back. He shoved his long legs out in front of him, crossing them at the ankles. "It's what I normally do. That's why taking care of the kids during the day won't mean much of a change in my routine." He smiled and folded his hands behind his head. "I'll simply have to get up a bit earlier, in order to get them to school on time."

He'd always been a night person, she remembered. And he'd loved sleeping in. In the few months they'd had together before Nathan was born, they'd both enjoyed staying in bed sometimes until noon on weekends.

"I can get them to school before I go to work," she said, "if you want to sleep longer." She surprised herself with the offer.

He surprised her by turning it down. "I said I'd take them to school and pick them up," he said firmly. "It won't hurt me to get up for that. In fact, it'll probably do me good."

"But you like to—"

"No. If you'd hired a nanny, getting the kids to school would have been part of her job."

"But she wouldn't have had to work in the evenings, like you do, to earn a living."

"Unless you had to be out late." He took another gulp of coffee before continuing. "Then, I suppose, she'd have been on duty." His dark eyes surveyed her from below half-closed lids. He smiled faintly, almost derisively, she thought. "Since I'm the new nanny, any time you have a date, Kat, just let me know. I'll stay with the kids."

She met his gaze levelly. "I'll ask you to be with them in the evening only if I have to work late. I see my social life as my responsibility, and I'll hire a sitter whenever I have a date. Unless, of course, it's your weekend with them. Then you'll have to hire a sitter if you want to go out."

He continued to gaze at her broodingly. "I heard you telling Katie that you'd go away when it was my weekend with them. I feel I might be crowding you out of your own home."

She shrugged and selected another cookie. "That's silly, Rand. There are plenty of places I can go. Plenty of people to go with."

Yeah, who? she asked herself. There was nobody in her life she would even consider going away with for a weekend. Not a man, at any rate, though Craig had been pressuring her to take in amateur dance competitions with him. A few months earlier she'd almost agreed to attend one in Seattle but backed out at the last minute. Something had told her he'd balk at separate hotel rooms. She wanted him only as a dance partner. Besides, she didn't think they were good enough to enter competitions. Now she and Rand . . .

"I suppose," he said, interrupting her thoughts, "your friend Todd can get free tickets to almost anywhere in the world." He sounded almost resentful.

"Yes." She supposed he could too. Maybe she'd even ask him about it one day.

"Where has he taken you so far?"

Kat frowned down at the cookie she still held. A chocolate chip had melted against her thumb. She licked it off. It became important, suddenly, that he know the truth. "Nowhere," she said, glancing at Rand. "We . . . don't have that sort of relationship."

His eyebrows lifted. "No? Then what kind of relationship do you have?"

"We're . . . friends."

"Is he gay?"

"No."

He looked perplexed. Kat sighed. She didn't think a man like Rand would understand her completely platonic friendship with Todd. Todd liked to balance his peripatetic lifestyle with having a family to visit. He was an honorary uncle to her kids, and something like a big brother for her.

"But don't worry," she said when Rand continued to regard her speculatively. "When it's your weekend, I'll make some kind of arrangements. I'll enjoy getting away."

"You don't have to," he said. "Unless you want to. You won't be in my way if you stay home, and I'll still take full responsibility for the kids. Get up with them in the mornings so you can sleep in, keep them entertained and out of your hair so you can rest. That sort of stuff."

"That—that will be fine," she said, knowing it would never work that way.

If she were on the scene, the kids would want to be with her. If somebody skinned a knee, they'd need Mommy, not Daddy. If somebody couldn't find something, it would be her they'd ask. And that, of course, was the way she'd want it. She'd hate it if he tried to keep them "out of her hair" and made them unhappy by doing so.

She'd hate it as much as she already hated the weekends and other times they went to stay with him. They were her babies. She loved them and missed them when they were away. And she longed, desperately, for the days when it had not been necessary.

As if he could read her mind, Rand startled her by saying, "We could maybe do something together. With the kids, of course. Sometimes."

"No!" she said swiftly, and turned back toward her desk. His feet prevented her from pulling her chair in close again. "I don't think so. We don't want to give them the wrong idea. About us, I mean. Since there is no 'us.' And that's another thing." She told him how easily the children could have misconstrued that little kiss over the breakfast table. "I absolutely do not want you kissing me in front of the children."

He grinned. "No? Then how about when they're not around?"

She set her jaw as she fixed him with an angry glare. "And not then, either."

"Whatever you say." As if the subject were closed forever, he straightened and leaned over, picked up one of her printout sheets, and scanned it. With a rueful expression he set it back down, clearly at a loss to decipher it.

"Tell me about your work," he said, his elbows on his knees, his coffee cup between his large hands. "What is it that keeps you busy all day and all evening too? You didn't used to bring paperwork home."

"Hardly," she said with a short, half-bitter laugh. "I can imagine what kind of reaction that would have gotten! It was bad enough that I had to neglect my wifely duties to go out and do surveys now and then."

A muscle jumped in his jaw, but he kept his tone even. "That was then, Kat. It's now I'm interested in. Tell me about your job."

Taken aback, and not a little ashamed of her snappishness, she shrugged. "There's not much to tell. My work hasn't changed a lot in two years."

"You said you'd had a couple of promotions. I take it you're still with Richardson Associates Research?"

She nodded warily. If anything could lead them into a fight, it would be a discussion of her job.

"What do those promotions mean to you?" he asked. "Have they changed your life in any way, besides gaining you a bigger paycheck? I know it's what you wanted, to climb the corporate ladder. Are you happy doing it?"

"Well, yes," she said cautiously. "For one thing I'm the head of my department." She couldn't hide the pride she felt. Lifting her chin, sitting a little straighter, she said, "I'm overall manager of the survey teams."

He looked impressed. "If I remember rightly, a department head at RAR carries the title vice president." He stood and grasped her right hand, giving it a quick shake. "Congratulations."

She pulled her hand back from his warm clasp. "Thank you. I'm amaz—" She bit off the rest of the sentence. If she and Rand were going to try to get along, try to talk, she was going to have to be mature enough not to take potshots at him.

He smiled down at her and lowered one hip to the edge of her desk. She wished he'd sit on the sofa again, or that she had enough room to stand up and move away from him.

Talk about getting in someone's way! He all but filled the space between her chair and her desk, leaving her no room to maneuver. She licked her lips and looked down, folding her hands tightly in her lap.

"You were going to say . . . ?" he prompted her.

She shook her head. "Nothing important."

He tilted her face up, gazed at her for a long moment, then shocked her by pulling her to her feet. Before she could protest, he'd swung her around and seated her on the sofa. Sitting beside her but mercifully not touching her, he said, "You're surprised I remembered that much about your company. You're surprised I was even paying enough attention to be aware of the different levels in their corporate structure."

She laughed. "I guess I shouldn't be surprised that you know exactly what I almost said. You know me too well, Rand."

"And at the same time, not nearly well enough. You, my—my lady, have changed in two years." He took her hand and held it loosely, rubbing his thumb over the backs of her fingers.

"I guess I have." She met his gaze for a moment. "But so have you."

"Yes. More than you might think."

She waited, but he didn't elaborate, merely squeezed her hand, then let it go. She continued to search his gaze, her mind whirling.

How had he changed? And how much credence could she give to those changes? If the differences she'd already noticed were real, something to rely on, were there others not yet evident? And if there were, what would it mean to their relationship?

The question scared her, set her insides to churning, made her throat hurt. If his changes were real, if he was no longer the philandering, cheating husband she had shed two years ago, were forgiving and forgetting suddenly possibilities?

Oh, who was she kidding? How many times had her mother forgiven and "forgotten," only to be forcibly reminded again, and again, and again?

"What exactly," Rand asked, "does the vice president in charge of the survey department do?"

Glad to have something concrete to focus on, she answered him quickly. "The head of surveys coordinates, collates, and interprets data brought in by the teams who go out into the field and ask the questions."

"What?" Amusement flickered in his eyes. "No more hanging around shopping malls demanding to interview total strangers? No more lurking in doctor's waiting rooms, or on school grounds, or collaring people coming out of the theater, to press your questionnaires on them?" His smile told her he wasn't making cracks about the long hours she'd once had to work.

"That's right," she said. "There are fewer hours of evening work." She smiled and glanced at her desk. "At least, evening work away from home."

He nodded slowly, his gaze intense yet unreadable. After draining his coffee cup, he set it down with a thump and stood. "That must give you more time for a social life, then."

Suddenly wary again, she agreed that it did. Standing also, she slipped past him and back into her chair. "Some." She stared at the printout he'd studied. It meant about as much to her at that moment as it had to him.

"Kat." She sensed him behind her. He placed his hands on the back of her chair and pressed down, tilting her backward until she was nearly lying flat. He looked at her, his upside-down image unsmiling. "I want to be part of that social life."

She stared at him, uncomfortably aware that her robe had ridden up her thighs. "No."

He tilted her back to an upright position, then swung her chair to face him. Crouching, he trapped her between his arms as he gripped the arms of the chair.

"It's inevitable," he said. "I won't be able to live this close to you and not want to . . . see you. You're not sleeping with Todd. Craig?"

Her breath got hung up in her throat. Her heart pounded high in her chest. "Rand, that's none of your business."

"You're my wife. That makes it my business."

"Ex-wife!"

His eyes flared. He leaned so close, his breath fanned hot across her face. "Words on paper. You're my woman, Kat. I'm your man."

"No," she said again.

He let go of the chair and caught her elbows instead, pressing them close to her body. His thumbs brushed against the undersides of her breasts. Her nipples responded instantly. His gaze dropped to them, then returned to her face. "No?" he whispered. "Your body's saying yes, Kat."

"What part of no don't you understand?" she asked in a taunting voice.

He shook his head and stood, releasing her.

"I know what no means, Katherine," he said with deliberate softness. She had to stay very still, listen intently to hear him, though his voice seemed to come from all around her. From outside her and within her all at the same time, accompanied by a strange roaring in her ears.

"But I also know that if I did this"—he bent and brushed his mouth over hers, once, twice, dry and hot—"as if I really meant it, or did this"—he stroked one hand down her shoulder and over her breast, a fingertip grazing her nipple—"your no would turn to a yes. Fast. Because," he went on, still in that soft, low voice, "I have something you want as much as I want you." He took her hand and pressed it to the hard bulge in the front of his jeans.

"Yours, Kat." His eyes burned into her soul. His voice became harsh. "All yours. All you have to do is say yes."

She snatched her hand back, clenched her fists so hard, her fingernails bit into her palms. Staring at him, her throat working, her heart threatening to explode, she was afraid of what he'd do next, and equally as afraid that he'd do nothing.

Which was what he did. He turned without another word and left her.

She buried her head in her arms on her desk. "I hate him! I hate him! I hate him!" she wept. "I'll have a lock installed on the kitchen door first thing tomorrow! And I'll never, ever, say yes."

But in the back of her mind, she heard her mother's weary voice as she tried to explain things to an angry daughter. "Never is a long time, Kat. You can lock the door as many times as you want, but when you love a man, you don't throw away the key."

"But I don't love him," she whispered. "I don't!"

Kat saw little of Rand over the weekend. Mercifully, she told herself. She sent Katie down to him when Todd arrived to pick Nathan and her up, spoke to Rand briefly when she got home, then watched his car pull out of the driveway at seven-thirty. She didn't hear it come back during the night.

Sunday, she glimpsed him in passing. He and another man were carrying a console TV with at least a thirty-inch screen down the basement stairs when she and the kids were on their way to church. When they returned, he was nowhere around, and she was nearly asleep that night when she heard the basement door open, then close quietly. The fourth step squeaked, and that was all she heard.

She rolled over, determined to sleep. Sleep was elusive, however, and when she eventually found it, it was heavy, unrestful. She was grateful not to have to take the kids to school when she got up in the morning. It gave her an extra half hour to get ready for work, not an easy task on Monday mornings at the best of times. For her, with Rand's presence in the basement suite like a disturbing, half-heard whisper of music she couldn't get out of her mind, it was not the best of times.

That night, she got home from work nearly an hour late and more tired than usual. Likely, she thought, because she'd slept so poorly the night before, thinking about Rand, about the things he'd said.

She sighed and hitched her bag of groceries onto her hip, fit her key into the front door, and unlocked it. From the family room she heard the TV blaring, heard Nathan's too-big voice booming at Rand to look at what he'd made, heard Katie's shrill laughter and Rand's deep chuckle blending in a strange harmony.

She closed the door quietly and leaned on it, glad to be home yet inordinately sad that the kids hadn't heard her key and come running to greet her. If they'd had a baby-sitter and she was late getting home from work, they'd have been at the window watching for her.

They'd have smothered her with kisses. They'd have been laughing with her, not someone else. Their joy at her return would have been as loud and enthusiastic as the pleasure they took in whatever they were doing with Rand.

Today, though, they didn't have a sitter. Today, they had their father, and judging by the continued merry racket, the three of them were having a whale of a time. Without her.

Well, why not? she asked herself, dumping her grocery bag on the kitchen counter. Rand wasn't a bored teenager who insisted on watching rock videos the kids hated. He was their father, and with him on the scene, what need did they have for their mother?

The question made her throat ache. The answer struck her like a blow to the solar plexus. They didn't need her. They hadn't missed her at all. They probably didn't even realize she was late!

So? How many times had she come home and wished she could crawl away all by herself, rather than having to deal with their needs? How many times had she thought longingly of a tub full of hot water and bubbles up to her ears? And blessed quiet. Why not snatch the opportunity to enjoy just that? Lord knew, after the day she'd just put in, she could do with a long, solitary soak.

"Hah," she muttered, kicking off her shoes. "Sure. A long, soothing bath any time between now and eleven o'clock isn't any more likely than a lasting friendship with Rand."

A stack of laundry big enough to sink the Alaska ferry awaited her, plus at least two hours of work going over the results of a consumer survey she hadn't had time to finish at the office. That last was largely due to the fact that she'd spent too many hours staring out the window with her thoughts anywhere but on her job.

As she stood looking down into the TV room, all three had their backs to her. A tidal wave of cut paper littered the coffee table and carpet. A multicolored stack of construction paper hung half off the couch, and an open box of macaroni lay beside it, some of its contents disappearing down between two cushions.

For several minutes Kat silently watched the three of them; then, as if sensing her presence, Rand looked over his shoulder at her. Swiftly, he got to his feet, spilling paper and bits of macaroni like a shower of confetti around him. A glue bottle dangled by its sticky nipple from the elbow of his shirt.

He picked it off, grinned, and said, "Hi, there," as if she were a neighbor he was greeting across the fence. He muted the TV and nudged Katie. "Mom's home."

Katie glanced up. "Oh, hi, Mommy. Daddy 'n' me are making a dinosaur." She waved a sheet of pale blue construction paper. On it a strangely shaped object was outlined with macaroni and filled in with bits of colored paper. "See?"

Kat leaned on the oak rail separating the kitchen from the sunken family room and admired the art-work with an enthusiasm she hoped didn't sound too false. Turning to Nathan, she asked how his day was. She got a shrug in return. He knelt by the coffee table, his dark hair hanging in his eyes, his tongue protruding from one corner of his mouth, his con-centration fully on the paper before him. When he finished, he held it up triumphantly. "See? A Sopwith Camel."

Kat squinted. "It looks like an airplane, Nathan."

Nathan and Rand shared a "women!" look, and Nathan said, "A Sopwith Camel *is* an airplane, Mom. Dad got me a book out of the library. It's got pictures of lots of really old kinds of planes. It's neat. And he got me one with helicopters, and another about dirub— drib— Dad? What are those things?"

"Dirigibles, Son."

"Yeah," Nathan said. "Those." He beamed at his father with hero-worshipful eyes.

"Come on, gang." Rand placed his hands on a pair of small bottoms and gave the kids gentle shoves into the middle of the mess. "Let's get this place cleaned up before your mother decides we can't play in here anymore."

To Kat's amazement, not to mention her irritation, the children set to without so much as a hint of argument or sulks. By the time she'd changed out of her suit and panty hose and unpacked the few groceries she'd brought home, the family room was perfectly tidy.

While they worked, the children pelted Rand with questions, dragged from the bottom of the toy box items he might not have seen, and left Kat to do her chores undisturbed. When not busy responding to the kids, Rand kept up a cheerful commentary about his day, seeming not to notice—or maybe not to care— that Kat's responses were subdued.

Coming to lean on Kat's hip for the first time that evening, Katie asked, "Can we have grilled-cheese sandwiches and tomato soup, Mommy?" It was her current favorite supper.

"Sure." Tired as she was, it was Kat's current favorite too.

"Okay, I'll leave you guys to it, then," Rand said so happily that Kat knew he was grateful not to be invited to join them. What man wanted soup and sandwiches for dinner?

She ought to be grateful she didn't have to consider a man's appetite when planning menus. She *was* grateful. Of course she was.

Kat picked at her meal while the children ate hungrily and chattered about the fun they'd had with their father. It sounded as if they'd packed a week's worth of excitement into the few hours they'd been together. Or maybe two years' worth.

After cleaning up the kitchen, she checked on Nathan, who was struggling over his math homework. "You have to carry the one, sweetheart," she said, bending over the coffee table where he knelt. "See, seven plus three makes ten. So you put down the zero part of the ten here, and write the one beside the other row of numbers, then add it to them."

He stabbed his pencil against the paper, making little holes. "Can you sit down and do it with me, Mommy?"

Kat thought of the mountain of laundry awaiting her. At that moment Katie yelled from the bathtub that she was ready to have her hair washed.

Kat sighed. "Could you wait till I wash Katie's hair?"

His lower lip jutted out. "I always got to wait. And you said I can't watch *The Simpsons* until I've finished this stuff. It's not fair. How come she gets her hair washed first? I asked first."

"Honey, I know, but if she waits, she'll get cold. She's all wet. I'll be right back, okay? In the meantime you keep on working, and you'll be done in time for *The Simpsons*."

He gave her a rebellious look and stabbed at his paper again. Katie splashed loudly in the tub. Kat left Nathan to his arithmetic and his sulks.

When she returned with Katie wrapped in towels, Nathan was gone from the family room. Kat frowned and called his name. He didn't answer.

She checked the rest of the house, though she *knew*. Pursing her lips, she flung open the door to the basement stairs and stomped down.

Rand answered her knock immediately, a pencil in his hand and a warm smile on his face.

Her voice was taut. "I can't find Nathan!"

Rand stepped out into the basement and shut the door to his suite. "Relax, will you? He's here."

She'd more than half expected him to be but still blew out an angry breath. "I told him to wait, that I'd be with him in a minute or two. He had no right to come down here and bother you."

"He's not bothering me. He wanted a bit of help with his math. Is it his bedtime?"

"No, it's not his bedtime. He didn't tell me he was leaving the house."

Rand frowned. "He wasn't leaving the house. He simply came down to see me."

"Dammit, I want him back upstairs right now!" She flung off the hand he reached out to placate her. "You have no right to let him stay down here when

Gold's tenancy. The overstuffed chintz sofa and chair remained, along with the glass-topped coffee table, all relics of garage sales—but good relics. Rand and Kat had fixed up the suite on a tight budget and rented it out before doing much to their own part of the house because the rental income would help pay their hefty mortgage.

Kat pursed her lips, remembering. . . .

SIX

The expensive split-level house had been too big for them, too upscale, but Rand had refused to listen to reason. He'd wanted that house, he'd wanted that neighborhood, and nothing else would satisfy him. The huge mortgage they'd been forced to sign for it was one he'd been determined to pay on his own, with no assistance from her.

"Stay home," he'd said when morning sickness had struck, rendering her all but incapable of moving before noon. "I don't want you to work anyway. It's a man's job to provide the home. Yours is keeping it. I'm an old-fashioned guy, Kat. Let me look after you."

At that time she'd had little choice, so sick had she been during her pregnancy. Then Nathan had been a colicky baby, and he'd needed her. Just when he reached an age when she might have gone back to work, Rand had suggested another baby.

Jenny had just had her youngest, triggering Kat's most female of instincts, to have an infant at her breast.

That, coupled with Rand's eagerness for another child, had tipped the balance. What difference, Kat had decided, would another year out of the job market make? Her boss at RAR had promised her a position whenever she wanted it, and she'd known he meant it.

And Rand, naturally, didn't mean it when he and Karl laughed and talked about keeping their wives barefoot and pregnant. He knew all along she meant to go back to work when the time was right, knew she valued her independence, her firm resolve never to be like her mother.

Kat's mother, Carol, had suffered terribly when her husband had walked out on her after seventeen years of marriage. Having never held a job outside her home, Carol had been ill equipped to look after herself and Kat, and their lives had not been easy through Kat's teen years.

Kat's second pregnancy was a breeze, and Katie a joy to take care of. When the baby was five months old, Kat's former boss called and begged her to come back. He needed her. Jenny agreed to baby-sit, and Kat went happily back to the office five days a week.

The happiness lasted until Rand returned from a three-week trip to eastern Europe. He'd known she meant to return to work, but until he actually lived with the situation, he didn't know how much he'd dislike it.

He wanted her to quit. She refused. She tried to explain that in her job, she felt useful again, that her mind needed something to do. Her days were filled with challenges and interesting people, not diapers and baby talk. She awoke in the morning with a lightness of spirit she'd lacked for too long. Besides, she felt uncomfortable never having money of her own, money she had earned. She hated feeling totally dependent on him.

He wondered if she was endowing him with her father's bad characteristics.

She suggested that he was trying to turn her into the woman his mother had been instead of letting her remain the woman he'd married.

He asked her again to quit.

She explained that her boss needed her.

He said he needed her.

She said he was never there long enough to need her.

He told her he was doing what he had to do to provide for his family.

She retorted that now the family had two good incomes, he didn't have to take foreign assignments.

He came back with the accusation that she was trying to undermine him.

She shouted that he was doing the same to her.

Their positions became so polarized that, after a while, no matter how hard they tried, they couldn't find the way back to any kind of understanding.

And they had tried, she recalled now, but it hadn't been enough.

Sighing from a surge of blended emotions, she stood and took a deep breath, drawing in the scent Rand imparted to the suite, so different from what it had been when Mrs. Gold lived there. Soap, shampoo, aftershave—essence of Rand—perfumed the air with a masculine muskiness that left her feeling warm and oddly dissatisfied. She prowled the room, touching his books, touching his CDs, touching his pictures of the children.

Through the open door of the room he'd chosen to sleep in, she saw the foot of his bed, a brown spread neatly squared on it, a pair of jeans flung across it. The rest of the room was in deep shadow. For an instant she was tempted to go in and see what kind of pictures, if any, he had in there.

No. That was none of her business. Besides, how would she feel if Rand came back and found her snooping?

She was glad she hadn't gone to investigate, because even as she was thinking about it, he came out of his workroom, still carrying the coffee she'd brought. He sipped it. "Cold. How's yours?" It, too, was cold, and he zapped both of them in the microwave.

She sat on the edge of the sofa again while he lolled back in his recliner, a mellowed-out tenant chatting with the landlady, an off-duty nanny conferring with his employer. An ex-husband waiting cagily to see what his former wife had in mind as a reason for this visit.

She half hid behind her coffee mug, looking at him through the steam. "I, uh, came to apologize for the way I acted over Nathan's coming to you for help with his arithmetic."

He leaned toward her. "Kat, you don't have to apologize to me for anything. I should have realized you might not know where he was. It was up to me to make sure he had your permission before I let him stay. I made that clear when I was tucking him in. He understands."

She shook her head and set her cup down on the end table. "No, he doesn't. And neither do you. I wasn't worried. If I hadn't found him with you, then I'd have been worried. What I was, Rand, was . . . jealous."

He stared at her over the rim of his brown pottery mug, that perplexed expression he and Katie both did so well—and so identically—drawing his brows together. "Jealous?" He sounded incredulous.

"Jealous." Her tone was flat, self-condemning. "You were all having so much fun when I came in this evening. I stood there for a good five minutes before anyone even noticed I was home. And then the kids acted as if they didn't care. It wasn't me they wanted, or my attention. It was you. It . . . hurt my feelings, and I've been in a lousy mood since then. I had no right to take it out on you. Or on Nathan."

"I see." He set his mug down and moved to sit beside her on the sofa. "Kat, listen. What this is, with the kids and me right now . . . it's sort of like a honeymoon. It won't last. And they do miss you."

She wasn't sure he was right, but she hoped he was. As they finished their coffee, he shrugged off her thanks for having done the laundry. "If you'd hired a nanny, she'd have done it, wouldn't she? I mean, when the kids are in school, what's a self-respecting nanny supposed to do?" He wrinkled his nose in distaste. "Watch soap operas?"

Kat conjured up a smile. "Not if that self-respecting nanny is named Rand Waddell," she conceded. "But you have cartoons to draw, writing to do. If you take time for laundry and things, you might get behind on your own work."

"I won't," he assured her. "And I want you to know, today wasn't just a flash in the pan, either. I started out this week the way I mean to go on. But I, uh, didn't touch your stuff, Kat."

"That's fine. It'll give me something to do with the rest of the evening after I've done my homework."

She made to get up, but he put a hand on her shoulder. "Do you have to go right away? There's something I've been thinking about. Something I want to say."

She sat back, and his hand fell away, but it felt as if it had left an imprint on her. "I guess a few more minutes won't hurt."

She waited for him to go on, but he only looked at her. His gaze seemed to be searching hers for something specific, though what, she couldn't guess.

"Kat . . . when we were married, when I was so hard to live with over your need to work outside the home . . . I've figured out what it was that bugged me so bad. I was jealous of you." He frowned, then shook his head. "No, jealous is the wrong word. I mean I was envious of your right to stay home. I figured you should revel in it, be grateful to me for making it possible. And all along, I guess what I really wanted was the right to do it myself."

Kat felt her eyes widen. "You—"

He held up a hand. "No, let me say it, now that I think I've finally got it sorted out. I'm happier working at home than I ever was going into the paper every day. Since I've been set up in my own space, I write more, I write better, and I write more easily. If ever a guy was cut out for this kind of life, I'm it."

She shook her head. "You as a homebody? I thought you *liked* going away. I thought that was your life—foreign trips, dangerous investigations." She lowered her eyes and stared into her empty mug. "I often thought you took assignments you didn't even have to take, just to get away from home. From me."

He lifted her chin and looked at her for a long, quiet moment. His dark eyes were grave and thoughtful. "There was an element of that the last couple of years. But it wasn't so much getting away from you, Kat, as getting away from the situation."

Before she could reply, he went on. "It was a situation I'd created as much as you had. If I'd had the insight then that I have now, I'd have realized how much better adapted I am to staying home and working alone than you are. You want people around. You require that stimulus. I don't. I'm better off working in solitude. If we'd figured that one out and compromised, we might have had a chance."

Kat's head spun so hard, she couldn't respond for several seconds. "You mean you'd have *liked* to stay home and keep house, mind the kids?"

He shrugged one shoulder, looking sheepish. "Yeah. I think so. As long as I'd had time to write and draw my cartoons, it wouldn't have mattered a damn where I did it. I've always liked being alone. When I was a kid, I spent more time in the library than I did anywhere else except school. I lived inside books. Fiction, fantasies of worlds I'd never know, places I thought I'd never see. They made life more . . . interesting. Oh, sure, I played hockey and football, because that's what boys do, and I had a lot of energy to burn up, but reading was what I preferred to anything. Reading about exotic people and places, so far outside my experience that I sometimes doubted they could be real."

It was such a rare glimpse into the childhood he never discussed that Kat held her breath, hoping he'd expand on it. He didn't.

"So travel was what you really craved," she said. "As I thought. That hardly ties in with being a house husband, Rand."

She saw something leap into his eyes, a denial, she thought. He opened his mouth to say something, then closed it again, shaking his head. "Maybe you're right. I'm not sure my ego would have let me become a house husband. Then."

"And now?"

He shrugged. "It's not complaining." At that moment his stomach growled loudly.

Kat raised her brows. "Something is."

"Yeah." He rubbed his flat, hard abdomen. He might spend most of his time over books, computer, drawing board, and other sedentary pursuits, but he still looked like an athlete to Kat. He probably worked out whenever his bad back permitted it. His ego, though it might have relaxed somewhat, wouldn't let him get too much out of shape. The spare tire, it seemed, had been wishful thinking on her part.

"Tell you what," he said, getting to his feet and pulling her up. "You go upstairs and get us some more of that good coffee of yours, and I'll make some cinnamon toast."

"Cinnamon toast . . ." Her mouth watered. It was a long time since she'd taken the trouble to make that as a snack. It was an even longer time since she'd shared it with Rand.

Feeling light-headed—or was that lighthearted?—
she nearly skipped up the stairs to get the coffeepot.

Maybe this was going to work after all.

And for those first couple of weeks, it did. It worked
very well. Kat and the kids and Rand settled into an
uneasy—at least for her—routine. He took the children
to school most mornings, picked them both up every
day, and she nearly always found them all together
outside when she arrived home in the late afternoon.
To her surprise, Rand did not only the laundry, but
the rest of the housework as well.

Sometimes in the evening they'd watch a movie
together if he'd rented one he thought she and the
kids would like. Sometimes, after the children were in
bed, the two of them watched something inappropriate
for children.

And they laughed. That was one area where Kat
felt they had made immense progress in learning how
to get along again. She was amazed at how easy it was
to share jokes with Rand, and she grieved for those
years when they had forgotten how. It was good having
that back.

The first time it was "his" weekend with the kids, he
took them camping. He didn't invite Kat. That Friday
afternoon, she watched them drive away in a rented
motor home that had plenty of room for one more
and felt as if she'd been abandoned.

She spent Saturday afternoon at the races with Todd,
and the evening at a dance with Craig. Sunday, she slept
in until nine, then rose and cleaned the house from top
to bottom, annoyed with herself for being annoyed that

it was already so clean. Rand had meant what he'd said about not being a flash in the pan.

Yup, she told herself. He'd shaped up as a great house husband. Too bad he was such a dead loss as a husband.

Frequently, she considered asking him to join them for dinner but refrained. It wouldn't be fair to the kids, raising their hopes, unless . . .

Unless what? Unless nothing. Because nothing was happening between them. If he'd meant what he said about being part of her "social life," he sure didn't appear ready to act on it. If he was waiting for her to say "yes," then he was displaying far more patience than he'd ever showed before. Not only that, he was asking nothing to which she could say yes. Not that it mattered, of course. "Yes" was the last thing she intended to say to Rand.

On a Monday morning toward the end of April, she walked the kids to school, then came back into the house for her purse and briefcase. Rand was waiting for her with a check, his child support payment for the month. She faced him across the kitchen table. "Since you're doing most of the chores," she said, "I'm not comfortable accepting child support from you any longer."

His eyes narrowed, and he slapped the check down on the table. She shoved it back toward him. "I'm serious about this. Keep it. Spend it on yourself for once."

She'd noticed he didn't have an extensive wardrobe, especially considering his bachelor status. She really hated to think of him doing without. "I know you're not having an easy time of it right now. When you're back on your feet financially, then we can reassess, but—"

"Dammit, I am having an easy time of it."

"Rand, please, you said—"

"No, I didn't! You concluded. I let you."

She backed up a step. "What?"

He jabbed a hand through his hair. "I let you come to a false conclusion. When I told you I'd started working at home, drawing a weekly cartoon and writing free lance, I also mentioned a column I'm doing. You may not have heard that, but I did say it."

She frowned, thinking back. The night she'd told him he could move into the suite, so much had been going on in her mind and her emotions, a lot of the finer details had become a blur. "I don't remember, but still . . ."

" 'Still' nothing," he said. "Columnists don't come cheap, Kat. I do an opinion piece. The publisher values my opinions, my writing. I have a substantial and growing audience. I write on foreign affairs."

She narrowed her gaze on him. That, she decided, sounded like a boast. "Really?" She made no effort to hide her doubt, her amusement. "How can you write intelligently on foreign affairs when you never go anywhere foreign, Rand? Surely, all your information must be about two years out of date."

His smile was lofty. "In a word, Katherine, contacts. Contacts with many people in many places, influential people who introduce me to other influential people. I keep in touch by modem, telephone, and fax machine. I may work at home, but I'm still out there in the real world as much as any man who hops a jet three times a week."

He paused for a moment, then went on with less adamancy. "That's why I'm not up some mornings in time to take the kids to school. Often I spend most of the night in communication with people in Europe, Asia, the Middle East."

She felt chastised. "Oh."

"My column," he added, "has been syndicated, so I have plenty of money."

Her jaw dropped. Syndicated? She knew what that meant in terms of money. She backed up another step. "You . . . lied to me?"

He had the grace to look mildly ashamed. "No. Not really. I—"

She released an explosive breath. "Yes, *really*. Not telling the truth is lying, Rand. I can't abide lies. You know that. You—"

"All right, dammit, I lied to you!" he shouted. "Give me a chance to explain."

She shook her head again. "You can't explain a lie satisfactorily. A lie just . . . is. And it's always wrong."

"Dammit . . ." Frustrated, he rammed his hand through his hair again. "Must you always see things black and white? Haven't you ever lied, say, to the kids, because telling them the truth was too difficult?"

She stared at the toes of her pumps. Yes, there had been times.

Rand moved closer to her. "And maybe what I said, or what I didn't say, wasn't so much of a lie, Kat." She looked at him. "Maybe, when you leaped to the conclusion that I was bankrupt, I really was, but in another way. I was bereft, not of money, but of a home, a family, and I wanted, very badly, to try to get it all back."

He saw doubt in her face, confusion in her eyes, and continued, lowering his voice, "Kat, please try to understand. I really, really wanted to be here. And my being 'destitute' seemed to be the only way you'd let me back in, so I jumped at it."

She worried her lower lip with her teeth. "Didn't you think I'd ever find out?"

"I knew you'd find out, because I meant to tell you as soon as you looked as if you were ready to admit this whole situation worked for the kids and for both of us. I should have come clean sooner, but there never seemed to be a good opportunity."

"Until now." She planted her fists on the table and fixed him with a steady gaze, a suspicious gaze. "Until I inflicted a wound on your ego by suggesting that you can't afford to pay support?"

He gave her a wary glance. "Well, yeah. I wouldn't have put it quite that way, but basically, that's right."

"Really." Her tone was flat. Her gray eyes held no discernible expression now. "Just how am I supposed to decide which statement is the truth, Rand? Do I simply take my pick?"

"I'm telling you which one is the truth," he said, his temper beginning to tick over now that he saw the direction her thoughts ran. "I lied about being broke. At least I let you believe—"

"Maybe you did," she interrupted, "and maybe you didn't. Maybe this last story of yours is all fiction. Maybe you're as poor as Mother Teresa and too proud to admit it. So I guess I just reach into the hat and pull out a choice." She went through the motions, reaching high and pretending to pick out a slip of paper.

"And the winner is . . . Rand Waddell, impecunious journalist, is still telling lies to his wife. Ex-wife." She smiled. "And I am still refusing your support check," she concluded airily, turning from him.

"Like hell you are!" he exploded. "Dammit, Katherine, that was never part of our agreement. I—"

"Have contributed plenty since you moved back here," she interrupted. "I don't want to argue about this, Rand." She picked up her briefcase, slung her purse strap over her shoulder, and headed for the door.

"Fine, then," he said, swinging the door open for her. "We'll forget you ever said it."

She came to a halt. "No. That's not what I meant. I mean, I don't want *you* to argue with *me* over it. Just keep your support check, bank it, do whatever you think is appropriate, but it's not going into my account any longer because I don't need it."

He glared at her, his jaw jutting out. "It will be on your kitchen table when you get home tonight, and will stay there until you bank it. And at the end of every month there'll be another just like it. Make no mistake about that. What you do with it is your business."

She raised her chin and glared right back. "I'll tear it up."

He tried to clamp down on the rage that threatened to overwhelm him. Her stubbornness had always been able to infuriate him almost beyond reason. "I'll deposit it in your savings account," he said between his teeth. "I know the number."

"I'll change my account number," she said, a pair of bright spots of color appearing on her cheeks.

"I'll find out what the new one is and keep on doing it every time you change it."

She blinked. "How could you possibly do that?"

He gave her a lordly look. "I," he said, "am damn good with a computer."

Her breath escaped rapidly, and he realized she'd actually bought his boast. "You'd hack into a bank?"

"If you force me to."

She sucked her breath back in. It lifted her breasts within the soft fabric of her blue blouse. Damn, but he liked her in blue. "Rand! That's against the law!"

He ground his teeth together. His eyes burned with the intensity of his frustration. Why did she have look so bloody appealing as well as be so stubborn?

Didn't she know the kids were out of the house? Didn't she know that the two of them were alone? Couldn't she sense that he was on the verge of taking her out of that prim blue blouse, that neatly tailored gray business suit, those proper dark leather pumps that made her look like such a lady? No. Maybe he'd leave those on her.

Didn't she know he wanted to tousle her, tumble her, tangle her in the sheets of his bed and keep her there for the rest of the day?

"And it's against my personal law for a man not to support his children," he said in an attempt to wrestle his mind back to the discussion before his imagination carried him away completely.

She sighed impatiently. "Very well, then." Her voice dripped ice, a challenging contrast to the fire in her eyes. Which was the real emotion? he wondered as his groin tightened. "Do what you must," she said, hitching her purse higher as she prepared to leave.

"Right." He grabbed the lapels of her jacket and planted his mouth over hers, sliding his tongue across the tight seam of her lips, then wooing his way in.

He felt the ice crack and melt and knew it had been only the thinnest of crusts. He heard her briefcase thud to the floor, felt her purse slither down along his thigh, then it, too, was gone. He captured her sigh, swallowed it, and enfolded her, rocking her from side to side as she grew soft and acquiescent in his arms.

Her arms clung around his neck. He kissed her again, deeply, tasting her sweetness overlaid with mint, feeling her heat, her softness. When he lifted his head and looked into her eyes, the fire of anger was gone, but he could see a banked heat simmering away.

She let her fingers filter through the hair at the back of his neck. "You need a haircut," she whispered.

He smiled. "Thanks. I must get one, then." He touched her lower lip with one finger.

"And you, my beautiful Kat, do what you must do. If you don't want my money, don't tell me about it. Bank it in the kids' names or something, but don't take my manhood away from me by denying my right to support them."

Kat tried to smile but only felt her lips tremble. Stepping out of the loosened cradle of his arms, she glanced down, then back up again. "If I took it away, Rand, you certainly got it back in a hurry."

Without shame he adjusted his pants in a futile attempt to make himself more comfortable.

"I'm sorry," she said. "I didn't know my refusing your money would hurt you. I didn't mean to do that."

He tucked behind her ear a piece of hair that had

come loose from the barrette at her nape. "Not supporting my family financially would make me a failure in my own eyes, Kat."

"I understand." Softly, almost shyly, she added, "You could never look like a failure in mine."

Before he could respond to that, she scooped up the briefcase and purse and all but ran from the house, as if afraid he might chase after her.

He hung on to the doorframe so he wouldn't.

Kat scurried to her car, climbed in, and locked the door, then felt foolish. She'd scared herself with the intensity of her response to Rand. It was crazy. She could not allow herself to be caught up in the sensual magic he could weave around her—around any woman.

He was a philanderer. A cheat. And, she reminded herself sternly, a liar, say whatever he might about merely having "let her draw a conclusion." If he'd wanted to, he could have told her the truth about his finances at any time. But he'd kept quiet for the sake of expediency.

He was not to be trusted.

But neither, she thought glumly as she drove away from the house, was her own overdeveloped libido.

The next time it was "her" weekend, Kat invited Todd, who had flown in that day, for dinner. She also made a point of letting Rand know she was having a guest.

"He likes the music loud," she said, "so if it bothers you, just hammer on your ceiling with a broom."

He shrugged and smiled and said not to worry because he probably wouldn't be in anyway. She forgot that later when, as she prepared to make the only dessert she felt competent to handle, she discovered she was missing a key ingredient.

"No flour?" She stared in disbelief at the empty canister, then slammed it back down on the counter. She remembered the liberal amounts Rand had used in making cookies with the kids. The nerve of him, using *her* ingredients to make cookies with *his* children! "How the hell can I make apple crumble without flour?"

She considered sending one of the kids downstairs to get some from their inconsiderate father, but they were both in their pajamas and bare feet, watching one last half-hour show before going to bed. Besides, as mad as she was, it would feel good to tear a strip off Rand.

Flinging open the kitchen door, she stomped to the landing and down the stairs to the basement. Her loud rapping elicited no response. She hammered again on his door.

About to wheel and charge back up the stairs, she grasped the knob and rattled it as she gave the door one last thumping to vent her ire. The knob twisted freely in her hand, and the door opened.

For a moment she hesitated. Should she?

Why not? Hadn't he made himself at home in her part of the house? That he'd done so because he was with the children might have some bearing on things, but she couldn't take the time to dwell on it or sort out the ethics of it. She needed flour, and she needed it now.

She entered.

Quickly, she helped herself to the cup of flour she needed, then almost ran to the door, caught by a panicky feeling that Rand would return at any moment and catch her there, thinking she was snooping into his private life.

She almost made it but stopped when she saw his old brown leather bomber jacket hanging on a coat tree near the door. She could scarcely believe he still had it, but then again, why not? He liked to hang on to things, she remembered as she unconsciously stroked a cracked, worn sleeve. "The pack-rat syndrome," she'd called it, smiling indulgently when one day he'd given her a peek into his past, showing her his "treasures," things left over from his warm and happy childhood.

As he'd showed her his reminders of the parents he'd lost when he was in his teens, he'd said little. Most of what she'd gleaned had been by inference only, by what he'd said he wanted from life, what he considered right and proper and normal in a marriage. His mother had been perfect—a regular June Cleaver—and his father presumably of the same ilk.

He hadn't brought many things forward from those days, not tangible things, but what he had, he'd valued—and clung to. She wondered if he'd opened his treasure box to show the kids the crackling, dry red paper heart with the lacy paper doily behind it. His mother had prized it because the six-year-old Rand had printed on it, *To my Valentine. I love you, Mom.*

And the brown leather jacket. That, she supposed, though he'd never actually said so, must have belonged to his father for him to treasure it so.

As she let her hand fall from the sleeve of the jacket and started to turn away, she did a double-take and gaped at the coat tree.

This was no memento of his childhood! She'd never seen it before. She'd never seen anything remotely like it! Now that she thought about it, she remembered seeing him carrying in a large, oddly shaped object a few days ago. It had been wrapped in heavy brown corrugated cardboard, tied securely with twine. She'd wondered at the time what it could possibly be.

She shook her head. Now, she knew.

She stared at it in horrified fascination, moving around to view it from all sides. By rights, she should be furious that he'd exposed her children to something so tawdry. She should be hiding it in the darkest corner of the basement.

But she wasn't. She was leaning on the doorframe, helpless with laughter.

SEVEN

Ornately carved and cast in bronze, the coat tree was comprised of three naked, full-breasted female figures shown from the waist up. Back to back, each held out its right arm, bent at wrist and elbow, to accept coats. Hats could perch on their left hands, which were held aloft in artful poses.

One woman had an eye closed in a lascivious wink. Another had her head cocked flirtatiously to one side while the tip of her tongue rested on her upper lip. The third, Kat saw when she lifted Rand's jacket down for the full view, had a sweet, angelic smile on her face. The middle finger of her right hand, though, was raised in a gesture so crude and so unmistakable, she was glad he'd covered it with his coat.

The thing was hideous. It was totally tacky. And exactly, she was sure, the kind of thing that would appeal to men. She was tempted to bring Todd downstairs when he came and show it to him, just to test her theory.

What a topic for a consumer survey: Would you buy an item like this? Would you want one as a gift? Would you give one as a gift? To whom would you give it? Why?

That was certainly a good question. *Why?* Why did Rand have it? And where in the world had he bought it? In some cheap secondhand store? Quickly, she hung his jacket back where she'd found it and opened the door. Then, turning back, she lifted his jacket and replaced it on the hand of the woman with the winking eye.

After giving the entire heavy coat tree a quarter-turn to the right, she left, still laughing, and went back upstairs to finish her baking.

Kat and Todd were playing a quiet game of Scrabble, with dance music playing softly on the stereo, when she heard the back door open and two sets of footsteps descend the basement stairs. "More coffee?" she asked, getting to her feet.

On her way to the kitchen she cranked up the volume of the music a notch and a half. It covered whatever sounds might have come from downstairs. She left it on even when Todd took his leave. Before she went to bed, she switched on the remote speakers that would flood her room with sound and never heard the back door open.

If it ever did.

"Hi, there."

Kat looked up from her weeding, shading her eyes

with a grubby hand as Rand loomed over her. "Hello," she said, keeping her voice cool to hide the sudden heat that surged through her.

He had no right to go around in disreputably tight cutoffs, bare feet and no shirt. His rumpled hair looked as if he'd just gotten out of bed. So did his eyes, all sleepy and half-shuttered, glittering darkly between his thick lashes. He squinted against the bright light.

He hadn't shaved and looked like a reprobate. Somehow all of that seemed sinful at nearly two-thirty on a Sunday afternoon.

It was also sinful the way her body responded to that kind of reminder of the past. Just looking at all that bristly stubble made her breasts burn and tingle as if he'd been kissing them. Her nipples puckered. He fixed his gaze on them, smiled. "Chilly?" he said. "I thought it was really warm for May."

She glared at him.

"I got your message," he added.

She shot to her feet, her arm shielding her breasts. "That was no message, and it was rude of you to mention it! You may think it's warm enough to go around half-naked, but I do find it chilly!"

"Why, Katherine," he said, grinning wolfishly, all shining white teeth and laughing eyes. "*That* wasn't the message I meant. I was talking about the message you left on my coat tree."

She sniffed, deciding that offense was the best defense. "Use up all my flour again and neglect to tell me, and I'll give you more than the finger, Waddle."

He compressed his lips, trying to look angry, and failed. "Don't call me 'Waddle,' " he said automatically. It was a battle she knew he'd fought all his life with little success. People still had trouble with his name. "It's Wad-*dell*."

"Then don't mess with my kitchen," she retorted, clenching her fists at her sides.

"I'm sorry." He looked anything but repentant. "I had no idea 'your' kitchen had become such an important factor in your life. I remember a day when you equated the word 'kitchen' with 'prison.' "

She couldn't help grinning at him. "I'd be just as mad if you took the bunk out of my cell."

He chuckled. "I meant to put flour on the list, but I couldn't find it, then it slipped my mind."

The list. Kat gritted her teeth. How she had hated that list! It had become a symbol of everything Rand had expected of her, everything she had failed to be. He had bought it for her, supposedly to make her life easier.

It was a small blackboard with a little ledge for chalk, and a list of all the staples every household might require printed on it. *Indelibly*. She was supposed to use the chalk to make tick marks opposite things she'd run out of, and to write down items that the list didn't contain. She'd always forgotten to fill it out, and she'd always run out of the key ingredients necessary for the smooth running of a household.

"Where is the list, Kat?"

"Gone," she said with immense satisfaction. "I threw it in the garbage. I, for one, don't find it necessary to keep relics of the past around to collect dust."

He took half a step back, his mouth tightening. "What makes you think that coat tree is a relic of my past?"

She blinked at the harshness of his tone. "The jacket, Rand, the jacket. Heavens, even I know that your late, lamented, and all-too perfect mother wouldn't have permitted such an item as that coatrack in her perfect household. I—"

She broke off, shook her head, and closed her eyes for a moment. Talk about a relic of the past. She had to learn to control her knee-jerk reactions.

"I'm sorry." She met his gaze, his simmering anger. "I shouldn't have said that. How—how was your date last night?" she asked to change the subject.

"Fine," he said, relaxing visibly with, she thought, as much self-control as she'd just exerted. "And yours?" He, too, seemed willing to make an attempt at amity.

"Just great."

He cleared his throat. "And it's a great day, isn't it? I've wasted too much of it, I see. I didn't get to sleep very early."

She clenched her teeth and crouched back down by the garden, ripping out handfuls of weeds. "I thought that, considering how late you slept. You did just get up?" She wasn't about to admit that she'd given a lot of thought as to why he'd failed to get to sleep.

He nodded. "About an hour ago. I had a couple of cups of coffee, a bite to eat, then watched a stock-car race on TV. Were you up early?"

"Early enough for church."

"Now, I feel really guilty. Need some help?"

"No." As if she'd said yes, he knelt beside her and began pulling weeds. As if she'd said yes, she let him.

They worked in silence for several minutes. "Was there enough flour for your needs?" he asked presently. "I was almost out too."

"I got what I needed." Her tone was curt, as she'd meant it to be, but her conscience poked at her until she said, "I'm sorry I went into your apartment uninvited, but, well, I knocked, then discovered the door was open, and I really needed flour for the dessert I was making."

He cocked an eyebrow. "You make desserts now?"

She shrugged. "Sometimes. Todd likes apple crumble. Since he was bringing the main course, squab and wild rice from a deli, I thought the least I could do was provide the salad and dessert."

His eyes hardened for a moment. "Dinner *à deux*, I assume, since the kids told me you were making tuna casserole for them."

"The kids were ready for bed when he got here, yes. He played with them for a few minutes, then we tucked them in and had dinner."

Rand's mouth flattened into a thin line. "And then you danced off your squab and wild rice? I—we heard your music."

She wished she could lie with ease, but she couldn't. "No."

She pulled a fistful of chickweed, shook the soil off its roots so violently that grit sprayed all around, then crammed it into an already overfull bushel basket. "Todd doesn't dance."

"That's too bad, since you love it so much. Hearing that music reminded me of the Saturday nights we spent dancing in the living room, just the two of us." He glanced sideways at her, his eyes soft. "During our impoverished days, before carpets."

She remembered too. Her hands fell idle in the weeds. "They were . . . happy times though," she said almost tentatively. Did he remember them as being happy? "When you were home."

He smiled, his gaze catching hers, "Yeah."

"You know, I don't recall feeling impoverished. But I was glad to get the place carpeted when we did."

"Even though it made dancing impossible?"

By the time they'd been able to have the house carpeted, Kat mused, after she'd been back at work for a year, they'd stopped dancing together anyway. Partly because his back had been too bad to risk that kind of movement, and partly because they'd grown too far apart.

"Any dancing I do at home now is done in the kitchen," she said to let him know subtly that she, for one, had resumed dancing, despite what she'd said about Todd. The kitchen was where she danced with the kids—frequently. They loved it as much as she did. "I'm sorry if I—we disturbed you unduly."

His larger, stronger hands made quick work of several thistles she'd been leaving to get out with a spade. "We weren't sleeping," he said cheerfully.

She said nothing.

"Where are the kids?"

"Katie's playing two houses over with her friend Parjeet, and Nathan's gone to a birthday party."

"So. We're all alone." He smiled teasingly. "Care to join me in the kitchen for a dance?"

Merely thinking of dancing with him made her throat tighten, her heart rate increase, and her mouth go dry. Her neck was too stiff for her even to shake her head. She could just see the two of them trying to dance. He'd take one turn around the room, then freeze into a position of acute agony as his back went into spasm; she'd be lucky if she got that far.

It had been a long time since the two of them had danced together, even been "all alone" together. The times they'd spent over coffee and conversation didn't count. The kids were close at hand then, even if asleep. She didn't quite know how to deal with him when the kids were both out of the house.

She also didn't know what to say to him.

If she said anything, for certain it would be the wrong thing, and they'd start flinging ugly words at each other. Either that, or he'd get up and stalk away. Not that his leaving would be so bad. It might be easier than his staying, easier than this uncomfortable, awkward silence that had fallen over the garden. Even the birds had stopped singing.

She wanted to look at him but didn't. What was he thinking, crouched there beside her? About the woman he'd been with last night, or about dancing with his wife years ago?

She jerked out a wad of wild cress, and Rand touched the back of her hand with one fingertip. "You should be wearing gloves."

She flicked his finger off her and took two crawling steps away on her knees. "They get in my way."

"Like I do?"

She dug up several crocus bulbs whose tops had withered and moved them to the back of the bed. They could mature undisturbed there, until she set them back out in the fall, to bloom again next spring. "I didn't say that."

"You're acting like I'm in your way."

"Well, this is your free weekend," she said, careful to modulate her tone, which had been too sharp.

"Shouldn't you be making the most of it, spending it doing something you enjoy?" *With someone whose company you enjoy?*

Or had he meant what he'd said earlier? Did he want, really want, to spend time with her? *Social* time? She knew he'd wanted sex with her. That, he hadn't made any attempt to hide. Indeed, he'd flaunted it, tormented her with it.

"I am spending it doing something I enjoy." He followed her lead, moving more crocuses, his care and tenderness with the small bulbs surprising her. "I enjoy this very much." He patted the soil around the limp, grassy leaves, then nipped off spent blooms.

"Gardening?" She looked at him. "Since when?"

He shot her a sideways glance. "Since . . . a while ago. It can be a very peaceful, companionable thing to do, preparing the soil for growing things."

"Companionable?" She'd only gardened alone or with the kids. She hadn't seen it as an activity to share. She couldn't see Craig getting his lawyerly hands dirty, and Todd wouldn't have the patience.

"It can be companionable," Rand said, "with a congenial partner."

"Really." She wondered whom he'd found to garden with. Congenially.

For several minutes, both were silent again. Then Rand said, "You don't seem very . . . companionable right now, Kat. You're ripping things out of there as if that's what you'd like to be doing to my hair. If you want me to go away and leave you to enjoy your garden in peace, say so, and I'll leave."

"It's just that I'm used to doing it alone," she said. "But if you want to work here, too, there's not much

I can say about it. After all, it's your garden as much as mine."

He clearly agreed, because he didn't leave. "What prompted you to add gardening to your other chores?" he asked. "I had no idea that you liked doing it, alone or otherwise."

"I never had time for it until— I never had time before."

"Until you didn't have to waste time on me," he said.

She gave him a hard look. "I didn't say *that*, either."

He sighed. "I know you didn't." He looked pensive. "I wonder if we'll ever be able to have a conversation without ending up sniping at each other. Except when the kids are present to act as a buffer."

She smiled ruefully. "Probably not, Rand."

"When did you decide to make flower beds back here?"

"The first summer we were apart." She remembered digging up a three-foot-wide, forty-foot-long section of lawn next to the back fence, remembered the bite of the shovel, the twist against her arms and shoulders as she turned the sod and soil.

"Sublimation," Jenny had called it, and she'd probably been right. Not that Kat was exactly missing sex with Rand. There'd been none to miss for several months before she'd packed up and left. She'd been too wounded, too angry, to respond to his overtures, and he'd given up trying.

But forcing a spade deep into the soil over and over with all her weight on her foot and leg, lifting, twisting, straining, had at least made her physically tired enough to sleep. There had also been satisfaction in watching small bedding plants grow and blossom. It had given her some kind of spiritual hope that life wouldn't always seem so bleak.

"I needed something," she said, "to keep me occupied the weekends the kids were with you."

"I've been thinking about that. It seems kind of dumb to stick to the weekend routine, now that I'm seeing the kids every day." He dumped a fistful of weeds into the basket, then used the little hand fork to work loose some deeper roots.

She glanced at him. "I think we should. I mean, we'd have to go back to family court to get it changed, and it hardly seems worth the trouble. Come September, Katie will be in school all day, and I may be able to make other arrangements for afterschool care."

His dark eyes took on a steely glint as his hands fell still in the warm soil. "Are you saying that I can only stay until then?"

Her brows knitted together. Was that what she was saying? "Not . . . necessarily," she said. "But I still think we should stick to our usual routine in case this situation changes. I mean, if one of us remarries, it wouldn't do for us to continue sharing a house, even though we live in completely separate areas of it. One of us would have to move out. Then the alternate weekend arrangement would need to apply again."

A muscle jumped in his jaw. "Are you planning on marrying again, Kat?"

"No. But . . . well, things can change, can't they?"

"I suppose so. But until and unless they do, why don't we come to a private agreement and simply decide that as long as I'm living here, we'll take each weekend as it comes."

"Well, all right." She reached over his idle hands and retrieved her digger. "We'll have to give each other a few days' notice, though," she added, "if one of us does decide to go away. In case our plans conflict. If I plan to go anywhere, I'll let you know by Tuesday afternoon."

He nodded. "Sounds fair enough." He got to his feet and emptied the basket into the wheelbarrow. When he brought it back, he crouched beside her again, his arm brushing hers as he reached across her for the trowel.

Suddenly, intensely, she wished he'd go away right now. Far away. For the rest of the weekend. For the rest of the year! It must be PMS time, because she had a terrible desire to lie down on the grass and cry.

"Don't you have something to do today?" she asked.

"Nothing at all." His tone was easy. "I always take Sundays off and loaf."

She'd noticed that, of course, over the past few weeks. Still, she said, "That's a change." For a supposedly home-loving man he'd once gone out of his way to avoid his home, even when he wasn't out of town. She sighed silently. She hadn't made home a particularly welcoming place for him, not after she'd gone back to work and been too tired all the time to work at her marriage too. If there was fault, blame, she had to share in it equally.

He rose up on his knees and tugged hard on some brown stalks of annuals she'd left from the previous summer. "I told you," he said. "I've changed. You admit that situations change, so why not people?"

"You shouldn't be doing that," she said, still feeling weepy and out of sorts. "You'll hurt your back."

He shook his head as he attacked some more of the coarser garden detritus. It wouldn't budge, so he stood and stabbed the large digging fork deep into the soil beside the root. "My back doesn't go out anymore."

She sat back on her heels and stared at his profile. "Why not? Did you have surgery or something?"

He smiled at her as the plant stalks came free. "No. I just learned how to live right."

She gave him a doubting look, then got to her feet to wheel the wheelbarrow to the compost box. On the way back she glanced at his bare back, glad there were no surgical scars to mar its perfection. There were just those three funny little freckles, forming a triangle under his right shoulder blade.

She wondered if any of his girlfriends remembered to kiss them from time to time, just to remind him they were there.

"Live right?" she repeated. "I suppose you mean not going to the newspaper every day, not jetting around the world. What does that have to do with back spasms?" she asked, crouching down again.

"Plenty. Once I learned some good relaxation techniques, they became a thing of the past."

"How nice." She wiped her hands on her jeans and unconsciously rubbed the back of her neck.

"Looks like you could use some of those same techniques," he said. "Want me to rub your neck?"

No! She almost shrieked the word at him but managed to say civilly, "I'm fine. But thank you for your concern."

He smiled at her. "You're welcome."

She made no reply, yet the silence in which they weeded seemed slightly less constrained after that.

"What caused this great change you feel has come over you?" she asked when the weeds in that particular bed had all been transferred to the bushel basket.

He smoothed the soil with his hands, then brushed some dirt off his fingers. "A variety of things," he said slowly, thoughtfully, not meeting her gaze. "Time, for one. For another—" He looked up. "I joined a divorced men's support group a few months after our split."

She stared at him in disbelief. Rand had never been much of a joiner. "You? A group?"

He shrugged, looking down at his hands.

Sitting on the grass cross-legged in the shade of a deodara tree, she gazed at him. He took a position in the sun, on the low stone wall surrounding the flower bed. "Why?" she asked quietly.

He shrugged again. "Someone suggested it."

Who? she wanted to ask. Some woman? "And you went?" She made no attempt to disguise her amazement.

"Yeah. Until I got used to it, I discovered that a little solitude went a long way, especially the kind that came after I'd finished my day's work. I figured joining the group would mean one evening a week when there was someone else around. Voices that didn't come from the television. People to talk to."

Kat swallowed hard. "I thought you'd have lots of . . . people to talk to."

He flicked a dark glance at her. "Women?"

She squared her chin and nodded.

He shook his head. "I wasn't in the mood."

"So you went to this . . . group." Jenny had talked her into trying something like that. She'd gone once and discovered about thirty women and three men discussing the difficulties of raising children alone. It hadn't been of much value. "What happened there?" she asked. "What did you do?"

Did twenty man-hungry women come on to you with different degrees of subtlety while the other ten pointedly ignored you?

"Not much," he said.

She smiled. "Sounds like the group I went to. Once. I was disappointed. Never went back."

"I wasn't disappointed because I'd figured it would be a waste of time except for providing companionship. I knew there was no way I could make myself air my dirty laundry in public. But I'd been assured I wouldn't have to say a word if I chose not to, that I could just sit and listen and no one would care."

So his hadn't been a group for single parents, as such. Maybe it was only custodial parents who got sent in that direction. But "air dirty laundry"? She wouldn't have liked that any better than he had. She waited for him to go on.

He gave her a small, uncomfortable smile. "I thought maybe I'd hear something that would help, if I listened to other guys' stories. Help me understand what had gone wrong with us." He picked up a pebble and bounced it on the palm of his hand, his focus on it. "And why. It didn't seem I had a hell of a lot more to lose, so I went."

More to lose? She'd thought he'd seen their breakup as a means of regaining his freedom. Had it been so bad for him, losing her? Had he hurt as much as she had?

She had never seen him as really wanting to understand what had gone wrong. As far as she could tell, she'd failed to be what he wanted. What she was hadn't been adequate for him. That being so, her leaving shouldn't have mattered very much.

Now, she had to wonder.

"Well, did it help?" she asked finally when he remained silent. "Listening, I mean."

"Yeah." He closed his fist over the pebble, again and again, rhythmically. "It helped all of us to realize that our problems weren't unique. To know that we weren't alone, that men need friends as much as women do. Friends, not necessarily sports or drinking buddies."

Well! She'd read about men's groups—a backlash against the feminist movement, they'd been called. Men getting in touch with their own feelings. "Did you, uh, meet out in the woods and beat drums?" she asked, genuinely curious, trying to picture Rand doing that. She failed.

He laughed shortly, a rasp of sound with little humor behind it. "No. We met in a musty-smelling church basement and beat our gums. We talked about our ex-wives, our kids, about visitation rights, and meeting support payments while trying to support ourselves."

He gave her an aggrieved look. "Some of the guys pay through the nose and never see their kids, you know."

"And the majority of divorced fathers," she said sharply, "never try to see their kids and never send a nickel to help support them. Don't ask me to feel sorry for divorced men as a class."

"Hey!" He held up a soil-stained hand, the pebble falling to the ground. It rolled against the toe of her sneaker. "I wasn't. And I know you're right."

She kicked the pebble away, and her temper subsided. "Sorry. And you've also been more than generous with child support."

"As you have been with access to the kids."

She managed a half-smile as she looked at him from behind a sweep of hair. "Quite the little mutual admiration society we've got going here."

He nodded and reached out to slide her hair back behind her ear, a gesture so casual and familiar, she noticed it only when it was done. With a sharp pang she wondered if things would have been different if they'd admired each other a little more openly during their marriage.

"What else does your group do?" she asked.

"You mean apart from sitting around grousing about our wives over endless cups of coffee, about how mistreated and misunderstood we all are?" He swatted a bug that landed on one of his magnificent shoulders and left a dirty handprint on himself. Had he left a streak on her face? No matter. He'd marked her in deeper ways than that.

"Apart from that," she said.

He seemed fascinated by his thumbnails and the dirt under them. "We sometimes meet in the churchyard and the cemetery attached and keep the grounds neat and tidy. Sort of by way of saying thanks." He glanced up at her. "That's where I learned to like gardening. Those are the people I garden with. As well as gripe with."

"Is that really what you do? Just gripe?"

"Well, no. Not now. Now, some of us have formed solid friendships, do things together, meet each other's girlfriends, wives, kids. We're sort of like a family in a way, those of us who've remained close.

"But at first we didn't do much more than moan. It was just what I'd expected, a bunch of guys getting together and belly-aching about how badly we'd been treated. Then, somehow, before I really noticed, we were asking ourselves why. Questioning whether we might have been wrong a time or two ourselves."

He gave a soft snort of self-derision. "It was a novel idea for most of us, let me tell you, but I slowly began to realize that maybe I hadn't been entirely fair to you, that maybe I should have been trying to see things from a different perspective. About that same time I also realized that I'd been had."

By her?

He smiled as if he read the question in her startled gaze. "By my friend. This wasn't simply another male gripe factory that had moved out of a bar or a locker room and into a church basement. It was counseling. The minister who met with us each week, and who was also going through a divorce, had been steering us in a quiet, unobtrusive manner, and pretty soon every one of us was thinking in ways we'd never thought before."

He grinned. "But don't get me wrong. We still crab about women."

She smiled faintly as she rubbed the mud off her hands onto the too-long grass. She'd have to get the mower out before she quit for the day. "Jenny and I used to do that over glasses of wine—we called our get-togethers whine-fests. We'd bitch about you and

Karl and your shortcomings. Unromantic husbands was the general theme of our sessions."

"Jenny griped?" Rand frowned. "But she and Karl had a perfect marriage. They had everything going for them. I never once heard Karl complain about Jen." He looked offended. "I didn't know she thought he wasn't romantic. I thought their sex life was terrific."

Kat stared at him. "Rand! For heaven's sake! Sex has nothing to do with being romantic."

He raised his brows. "No? What *does* have to do with being romantic, then? In what way did Jenny find Karl unromantic?"

Before she could reply, he shook his head. "No. No, dammit, you said unromantic 'husbands'—plural, meaning me too. So let's put the real issue on the table here, Katherine. In what ways did you find *me* unromantic?"

EIGHT

Kat did not want to answer that question. Why couldn't he have simply stuck to the subject, which had been Jenny and Karl and their marriage?

"Rand. Please, let's drop it. It's the past. We have to let it go."

He slipped off the wall and clamped his large, dirty hands over her shoulders, giving her a quick shake. "No, I can't let it go. Don't you understand that, Kat? I've tried, but I cannot. Please, for God's sake, once and for all, tell me where I started to go wrong!"

"Don't," she implored him. "It wasn't all your fault. You know that. It took both of us to 'go wrong.' And we did. Most ways."

"Stick to the subject," he said, giving her another little shake. "You said I was unromantic. You never, no matter how many other things you said, and there were plenty, called me that. If I was, why didn't you tell me?"

She bit her lip, sighing. "Because it wasn't one of

the big issues, Rand. It was something I didn't like, but it was also something I could live with. No husband is perfect, just as no wife is. And since Jenny and I both had unromantic husbands, we could complain to each other about it. There was no need to tell you."

He closed his eyes for a moment, then released her and sat back down on the stone wall. "Maybe not," he said. "But my not being romantic enough . . . that surely was something fixable. If you'd told me."

She plucked at the grass. "I couldn't, Rand. Not really. I mean, if a man does romantic things because he's been asked to, then it's not very romantic."

A look of deep despair crossed his face. "It seems a guy can't win. But even it wouldn't have helped then, my knowing what you wanted from me in that way, maybe it'll help in the future. Tell me, Kat, please?"

What future? she wondered. Or, rather, his future with whom? She shrugged away a stab of pain. Why not tell him? It couldn't change anything, but it couldn't hurt, either.

"You gave me things like place mats for Mother's Day, and seat covers for my car on my twenty-seventh birthday, butcher knives another time. Lots of stuff like that."

He frowned. "I remember those seat covers. You said you needed them."

"I did. I'd been hoping we could find room in the budget for them, since there was no money for a new car, but I didn't want them for my birthday. I'd had my heart set on a green silk caftan that year."

She saw a look of distress cross his face and wondered if he was remembering other unromantic gifts he'd given her, like that unbearable kitchen list.

"Why didn't you tell me what you wanted?"

"I thought I had, subtly. Several times we'd walked by the store window where the caftan was displayed, and I always said how pretty I thought it was. You agreed, and I was sure you'd buy it."

A small chuckle escaped her. "I thought you were playing tricks on me when you gave me that big, heavy box that couldn't possibly contain anything made of filmy silk."

She smiled wryly at the memory. "But you weren't, and I had to pretend to be thrilled with seat covers."

He shook his head. "I'm sorry, Kat. Really, really sorry, but if you didn't like what I gave you, wouldn't it have been better to tell me than to gripe to Jen about it? Or if you wanted that silk thing, why didn't you go out and get it yourself?"

Rand really wanted an answer, but she didn't give him one. She just leaned forward and clasped her ankles with her hands, staring down at the grass. A hummingbird dive-bombed her hair, attracted by its bright color. He shooed it away gently, remembering how much she liked the little iridescent green darting creatures, how she'd rejoiced every March when they returned from their Mexican winter.

She liked all pretty things. Why hadn't he remembered that when it came to buying gifts? He felt lower than a snake. She hadn't bought pretty things for herself because, whether he liked it or not, her paycheck had been eaten up by necessities. Such as shoes for kids who seemed to grow out of them almost every other week, by the huge mortgage his pride had saddled them with. Her pay, his pay, every bit of it had been earmarked before it was earned. He hadn't been able to do it all on his own but had been too stubborn and proud to admit it.

"Kat?" he said quietly. "I wish you'd told me. I'd have bought it for you, that caftan. You would have looked pretty in it. Like a hummingbird. And since I was too stupid to know that you wanted it, you should have gone out and bought it yourself. You should have been able to enjoy some of your earnings."

She lifted her head. "I enjoyed lots of things," she said. "But . . . silk caftans aren't something a woman buys for herself. Not when other things are more important. Besides, I wanted you to think of romantic gifts on your own, because you *felt* romantic about me, not because I told you you should."

He picked up the small garden fork and fiddled with it. "If you didn't tell me, how could I know?"

"I'm not sure. Maybe we women expect our husbands to be mind readers. I know that's not fair. But a woman wants to be treated like more than a household convenience. She finds it insulting when her husband forgets that she's a woman first, a housewife second."

"I see."

Kat smiled suddenly. "Probably not," she said, "but it's okay."

Oddly, after all this time, it *was* okay. Sure, someday she'd like to be treated like a queen—at least part of the time—but she and Jenny had often agreed that they didn't really have it so bad. It could have been a lot worse.

It had gotten a lot worse. For her.

He shook his head as he looked at her. "No, it's not okay, Kat. I'm still not sure why it's not right for a man to give his wife something she needs, something to make her life easier.

"I distinctly remember your getting mad one day and flinging a cheap, dull butcher knife in the sink because it wouldn't stay sharpened. That's why I bought you that good set in the wooden block. I suppose you hated that too?"

She uncrossed her legs and got to her feet, rubbing her hands up and down her arms. The spring afternoon had begun to cool. "I didn't hate the knives, Rand, or the seat covers. I just didn't . . . treasure them as I might have other things. I wanted you to give me pretty things, delicate, feminine things, that you'd enjoy seeing me wear because you . . . loved me.

"I wanted you to see me, to think of me, as a beautiful, sexy woman with a body you were pleased to adorn with beautiful, sexy garments—for your pleasure as well as mine.

"When you gave me impersonal gifts, household things, it made me feel that you thought of me not as a woman, not as your lover, but as nothing more than a wife and mother."

Rand stood too. "You *were* a wife and a mother." His eyes showed his hurt and bewilderment. "What's wrong with a man thinking of his wife like that? A wife and mother is the greatest thing a woman can be!"

Like his mother, Kat thought despairingly. This entire discussion probably made no sense to Rand. Still, something kept her at it. "Maybe so," she persisted. "But she wants her husband to value her in other ways too."

He blew out a frustrated breath. "But I did val—" He broke off. "If a guy wanted nothing more than a lover, he'd never bother getting married. Lovers are a dime a dozen. I thought women didn't want to be seen as sex objects, for cripes sake! A man's wife is somebody special, important in so many ways. She—"

He broke off again, rammed his grubby hand through his hair, and went on. "When I bought you stuff you decided was impersonal, I wasn't insulting your sexiness, but honoring you, paying respect to your position as the mother of my children."

"I understand that," she said, then added, smiling faintly, "I think. But what men sometimes don't understand is that we women don't always see the position as mother of a man's children as the ultimate reward."

"*Jenny* did!" he said, raising his voice. "Jenny was proud of being a wife and mother, remember? She did see it as the ultimate reward. She liked staying home. She liked raising kids." His face twisted. "Hell, she liked it so much, she even took on the task of raising ours."

"That's not fair!" Kat was aware she was shouting. She didn't care. "She wasn't 'raising' ours, Rand! She merely took care of them while I was at work. When I was at home, I did the rest of it. *All* the rest of it," she added pointedly, to remind him of how seldom he'd pitched in and done his share.

He stepped in close, too close, his body heat reaching out to her. "She toilet-trained Katie!" he roared. "She taught her how to drink from a cup. She was there, not you, when Katie took her first step."

White heat infused Kat. "And I was there, not you, when both our children were born, Rand. So don't speak to me of neglect." With both dirty hands she shoved him. "Get out of my way, Waddle! Get out of my sight!"

She spun and would have strode away, but he caught her elbow and whirled her back. "I told you not to call me that! You know I hate it! *Miss Butts.*"

Kat's fury died as swiftly as it had risen. She covered her face with one hand. "Oh, dear Lord." She shook her head. "What are we doing? I'm sorry I called you that. It was childish and . . ." A small rueful laugh escaped her as she lifted her eyes to look at him. "It was just plain immature. You called me neglectful, and I saw red."

His tight grip on her elbow relaxed, but he didn't release her. "I wasn't accusing you of neglect, Kat. Simply of . . . not being there enough."

"And I was pointing out that neither were you. For them. Or for me."

"But I was trying to earn a liv—" He broke off, swallowing with difficulty, and she watched the high color recede from his face. "You're right," he said after a moment. "I'm sorry."

She searched his eyes and saw that he was sorry, but she wasn't sure for what exactly.

She nodded. "It's all right."

He slid his hand down her arm until their fingers were linked. She stared at them, at her nails, caked with dirt, at his, much the same. It was a strange sight, because of the dirt and because of the togetherness. They hadn't done anything together for a long time. They had never dug in the soil side by side. And for a brief time it *had* been companionable.

Then they'd started talking.

As if he wanted to recapture the moments when they had spoken as friends, Rand lifted their linked hands and brushed her dirty knuckles under the side of his jaw. "Would you . . . would you like to go for a walk or . . . something with me, Kat?"

For a moment she hesitated, then shook her head and pulled her hand free. "No. I've had enough sun for one afternoon."

She saw his jaw tighten as he glanced around the now half-shaded yard and back at her. Okay, so she hadn't had all that much sun, and it was nothing more than an excuse. She couldn't help it. There really wasn't anything more to say. "Thanks for your help in the garden. I, uh, excuse me."

"Sure," he said, and let her go.

Rand watched Kat's stiff back and shoulders as she marched into the house, and he sighed. One step forward, one step back? Or had it been merely half a step back? Dammit, why couldn't he keep his big mouth shut? He frowned. And why had he never thought to tell Kat he was glad she was his lover as well as his wife and the mother of his children? Or found a way to show her?

Because he'd thought her being his wife was so much more important? Well, yes, he had. He couldn't help that. Some things a guy couldn't change. He'd been glad she'd married him, proud. It had made him feel like a hero, knowing she carried his child, knowing she needed him.

But had he given her what she needed? Or had he given her what *he* thought she needed? He remembered her saying, the day she agreed he could live in the suite, that he'd wanted what he thought she should be, but that the reality of her had been wrong for him.

He thought of the things he'd bought for her, stupid, unromantic gifts. Had he been buying them for that fantasy she'd accused him of creating out of his need? Yes, maybe he had. But, dammit, money had been tight. She'd needed good sharp butcher knives more than she'd needed sexy nighties.

If only he'd realized long ago that she hadn't wanted practical things. They clearly hadn't told her he valued her in every way, especially in the ways she wanted to be valued. He wished she'd told him so. He wished he'd been perceptive enough to figure it out for himself.

Frowning, he walked inside the house, pausing to scrub his hands at the laundry-room sink. Sitting on the windowsill above the sink were her two rings.

He'd wanted her to have that diamond, and it had been impractical as hell. He'd wanted to give her one before they got married, to show the world that she belonged to him, but he hadn't had the money for it after making the huge down payment the house had required.

Had she felt cheated out of something special, denied an engagement ring as well as an engagement? They hadn't even had a white wedding. Things had been too rushed, and besides, neither of them had any family. For that matter, they hadn't had many friends, not locally. She'd moved to the Lower Mainland from the Kootenays, he from Yukon Territory, shortly before they met.

They'd married in the office of a marriage commissioner in a ceremony that took all of five minutes. Had her feminine, romantic heart mourned that loss too?

He remembered how her eyes had shone when she'd opened the jeweler's box and seen the diamond ring he'd bought her for their first anniversary, recalled how tears had shimmered in them. Her lips had parted in a tremulous smile, and she'd sighed his name.

Then she'd said, "You shouldn't have," and he'd told her he knew he shouldn't have spent the money so foolishly, but that he figured she'd earned it. "You gave me a great little son," he'd said. "You deserve a reward for being such a wonderful mother."

She'd hesitated, then said that they could have done with some furniture to fill their big, empty living room but had thanked him again. He remembered noticing that the radiance had drained from her face, and the smile on her lips had been forced.

What had she really wanted? he wondered. For him to say that he'd bought it simply because he loved her? Because he thought her pretty hands deserved decoration? He did love her; she knew that. And he did think that about her hands, but he'd have felt uncomfortable saying so. In light of what she'd said today, though, he realized it must have been what she wanted.

She'd probably have loved to be showered with diamonds, with furs, with silks and satins and all that, and done without carpets on the floors. Pretty lingerie so she'd know he still found her sexy.

He sighed. Maybe it would have been nice, slowly stripping off a satin gown, but mostly the two of them had slept in the raw, except when the babies were small. At that time she'd slept in one of his Tshirts in the summer, and something warm enough in the winter for her to get up and tend them in the night.

He shut off the water and stood there, listening to the singing in the pipes as she showered, thinking of her as she would be at that moment, smooth and sleek and wet, beads of water running over her body. He visualized her hands, slick with soapy bubbles, rubbing over her skin.

He groaned and gripped the rim of the laundry tub. As a lover, she'd been more than he could have asked. But had he ever reminded her of that, after the kids were born?

He ached to go to her right that minute and make it abundantly clear.

Get out of this house, he said silently. Go for that walk by yourself. Go for a drive. Go jump off a cliff! Just stop fantasizing about her. Stop remembering.

Her shower shut off. He stared out the window at the garden bed where they had spent a mostly companionable time working together in the warm soil, under the warm sun. He wondered what she wanted to plant there. Whatever it was, he'd go out tomorrow and buy it, then they could plant it together in the evening as the sun went down.

Flowers. Flowers were a romantic gift. When was the last time he'd bought Kat flowers? Lord! When Katie was born. He'd had them sent because he was away at the time. They were long dead before he got home, so he never even knew what the florist had chosen on his behalf. Or cared enough to ask. Yes, tomorrow he'd buy a bunch of flowers for them to plant together. How about some roses?

Maybe they'd manage to talk a little more, too, the way they had today, getting at some real issues instead of just skimming the surface.

He stood for some time, thinking about the past, about what they might talk about tomorrow, about a possible future for them. He was about to turn and go downstairs to his suite when a soft sound drew his attention. Turning from the window, he cocked his head, listening. He didn't know exactly what he heard, but he was disturbed by it nevertheless.

On silent, bare feet he padded across the cool kitchen tiles and glanced down into the family room. He saw nothing and turned to the hallway. A shadow on the wall of the stairwell moved slightly, and he took a step that way.

Kat! Sitting on the stairs, her head on her knees, crying.

Kat left Rand outside and strode quickly into the house, pausing in the laundry room to wash her hands and arms in the concrete tub and kick off her muddy gardening shoes. She started to pick up her wedding band and the diamond ring that didn't quite match it, then pulled her hand back and left them there on the windowsill.

Maybe, she thought as she ran upstairs to her room, Darinder, Parjeet's mother, would have a pot of coffee on. Darinder's husband was working that weekend. Some purely woman talk would be heavenly right about now.

A wave of grief washed over her as she longed for Jenny's friendship.

Jenny would have known what to do about this situation.

Kat had showered and dressed in pink leggings and a white cotton cardigan when it occurred to her that if Jenny were still on this earth, still there to look after the kids, the situation wouldn't exist.

"Jenny," she said as she left her bedroom, "sometimes I get so mad at you for getting killed, I could just spit!" As if Jenny had spoken aloud, she heard her friend's voice saying, *Hey, Kat, come on, let's be grateful. Maybe we don't have romantic husbands, but let's think of all the good things we do have.* So often Jenny had laughingly ended their whine-fests on that note.

Kat tried. She sat down on the stairs, pressed the heels of her hands to her stinging eyes, and tried. But it was so hard. How could she be grateful when life had deprived her of so much? Including the dear friend she needed right now.

She rubbed her eyes, surprised to find that tears had overflowed. She wiped them carefully on the cuff of her sweater, but little streaks of mascara were still left on the ribbed cotton. It wouldn't do for her to get to Darinder's house and have Katie see that she'd been crying. It was so stupid to cry at this late date anyhow. Her marriage was over, but she had two beautiful children to show for it. Two kids and a name far preferable to "Butts." She should be grateful. She should not be in tears.

But they simply wouldn't stop. Huge, choking sobs rose up in her chest, creating a tight ache that could be relieved only in releasing them. Silently, laying her head on her knees, she let them come.

Jenny, Jenny, where are you? Whom could a woman go to for solace and advice when her best friend just up and died on her? Loneliness was like a lid pressing down on her, more than she could bear. Oh, God, Jenny! Why?

"Baby, baby, what's wrong?"

"Jenny," she cried. "I want so badly to talk to Jenny! I need to, Rand! I really, really need to! Why did she have to go and die just when I needed her most? I haven't got anybody! I need someone, Rand. So much. I have to talk to someone."

It seemed so right, she thought, as he pulled her into his arms and held her. She pressed her face against his bare chest, wrapped her arms around his torso, and bawled.

"Talk to me, Kat," he crooned. "Talk to me. I'm here."

"How can I talk to you when it's you I need to talk *about*?" she wailed.

"Who better?" he asked, but she didn't answer. He didn't think she'd heard him. She only wept while he continued to hold her, cradling her, loving the smell of her hair, the feel of her warm body in his arms. When he picked her up and stood, carrying her to the sofa in the family room, she burrowed her wet face into the crook of his shoulder.

After she'd cried herself out, she sat motionless on his lap, her face still pressed to him. Her hands lay still and loose, one on his chest, the other on his waist. Her breath came in shuddering little sighs, as if she didn't have it completely under control yet. She sniffled wetly, and he stretched out an arm to reach a tissue from a box nearby. He tucked it into her hand, and she took it and blew her nose.

He got another and wiped her face, though she refused to lift it and let him look, going all stiff and resistant when he tried. He remembered how she hated to have him see her when she'd been crying and let her be.

He stroked her back, her neck, her hair, saying nothing.

Presently, she whispered, "I'm sorry."

"What for?"

"Inflicting this on you. Dammit, it's been months. I should be getting over it by now."

"How long did it take you to get over losing your mother?"

"Years," she said. "But that was different. When she died, I was twenty. I'm older now, a mother myself. I should be able to handle grief better. I was more of a basket case after their funeral than after my mom's."

"I wanted to sit with you at the funeral," he said. "I . . . wanted to hold you. Help you through it." He swallowed the thickness in his throat. "I could have done with a bit of help, too, I guess."

Kat recalled the dark-haired woman sitting next to Rand in one of the front pews. She'd thought he had someone to help him get through it. But maybe he meant someone who had known Jenny and Karl and their kids.

"I don't think we could have helped each other much," she said. "It might even have made it worse. Jenny wanted us to get back together. Almost as much as the kids did."

"I know."

Kat sighed, knowing she should sit up, move away. She wanted to, yet she needed to lean on Rand, if just for a few minutes more. It had been so long since she'd felt this . . . cherished.

Rand slid a hand through her hair, down over her neck, where he rubbed gently with thumb and forefinger. Her skin was warm and slightly damp. She smelled of soap and shampoo and her own inimitable scent.

She tensed, and he said quickly, "I was thinking of Jen and Karl just the other day, remembering the fun weekend we had when both sets of their parents arrived unexpectedly at the same time."

It had been just after the birth of Karl and Jenny's first child, Colleen. She'd been a first granddaughter on both sides, and had four very excited grandparents. Rand and Kat had offered overflow sleeping accommodations, and had hence been included in all the family festivities. They'd enjoyed being part of a three-generation gathering, especially since neither had parents of their own.

Kat smiled. "And remember how they ran out of Halloween treats to shell out, and Jenny and her mom put on sheets to make the rounds of the neighborhood."

Rand laughed huskily. "Right. Hey, remember when . . ."

For an hour they sat together, reminiscing about Jenny and Karl and their children. Sometimes Kat's tears welled up again, and Rand gave her fresh tissues. Sometimes, he'd tip his head up and stare at the ceiling, unable to speak for a moment, and she'd pretend not to notice.

At length, though, she pushed herself off his lap and slid to the far end of the sofa, head hanging low, hair providing a cover for her poor, blotchy face.

"Rand . . ."

"Yeah?"

"Thank you. That helped, you know. Talking about them like that. Remembering the good times."

"Helped me too." His tone was raspy. She got to her feet and moved a couple of paces away. He came to stand behind her. She felt the heat of him on her back, then his hands on her shoulders. He turned her.

She kept her head down even when he placed both hands around her neck, his thumbs under her chin, urging her face up. "Don't," she whispered. "I don't want you to look at me. I look like hell."

"I don't want to look at you," he said. "I only want to kiss you. I have my eyes closed." There was a hint of laughter in his voice, and she let him tilt her face up. She risked a peek between swollen lids. He did have his eyes shut. His thick black lashes lay on his cheeks, fluttering slightly.

Even with his eyes closed, he found her mouth with unerring accuracy, and she felt a shudder course through her. It was answered by the one that shook him as he wrapped his arms around her and drew her firmly into his embrace.

Sighing, she lifted her hands and put them on his shoulders, then slid them around and linked them behind his neck. She accepted his mouth on hers, moving her lips against his, tasting him.

Was this part of the mutual healing they'd begun, grief therapy to help each other adapt to the loss of their friends, or was it something else? Kat didn't know, but she knew she needed it as much as she had needed to weep in his arms.

It was a gentle kiss, nothing more at first than their

lips brushing together, the tips of their tongues touching in tantalizing little flickers. Her stomach fluttered with sensations she'd all but forgotten as their bodies came together. Her muscles contracted, tightening in hot spasms deep inside. She felt another sob rising in her chest, a different kind, though, from a different cause. She choked it down and heard it escape as a tiny, soft whimper of need.

His need must have been as great, because without further hesitation, his mouth was suddenly hard and seeking, hot and demanding, his hands molding her to him. As he parted her lips with his tongue, plunging inside, she gripped his shoulders, then slipped her arms around his chest, clinging to him, fingers digging into his back.

He pushed one leg between hers and flattened his hands on her buttocks. His hardness tempted her, urged her to rise up to him, made her strain to get closer. He moved her seductively against his body, drawing a long, shaky moan from her.

When he lifted his head finally, her breath was coming in short little spurts. "Rand," she said. "Rand . . . Oh."

"'Oh' is right. I . . ." He said no more, just held her, his cheek, all bristly and rough, pressed against her temple. She drew in his scent, slightly sweaty from his work in the garden, earthy and totally appealing. Under her hand, she felt his heart hammering so hard, she thought it had to be dangerous for him. Too bad. *He* was dangerous for her.

She dropped her face down and kissed the streaks her tears had left on his chest, then licked at the salt.

He dragged in a shuddering breath. "Kat..." It was a warning.

She stopped, and he pressed her cheek to his bare skin. She let it rest there, trying to memorize exactly how it felt for the times in the future when she would forget how good it could be, being close to Rand.

When he moved his hand, she thought that he was about to break their embrace, that he would step back. Instead, he tangled his hand in her hair, murmured her name, and brought his mouth down onto hers again.

Her head swam as they kissed, desperately needful, yearning for something lost . . . and maybe found again. Had anyone ever kissed her like Rand did? He put everything he had, everything he was, into his kisses. Deep, rich, voluptuous, they could turn a woman inside out in only a moment.

She ran her tongue over the inner side of his lower lip, tasting his unique flavor, reveling in it. He did the same to her, asking this time. She opened for him, and he entered, stroking, retreating, then returning as if compelled.

As she was compelled. She burned where he touched her. She ached where he didn't. She went soft and liquid, and a long, trembling moan escaped her as her knees turned to butter. As she dug her hands into his thick hair, he pressed his knee between her legs, sliding his thigh against her. Her body moved in time with the rhythm of his hands on her backside, and he groaned again and clasped her buttocks more tightly, lifting her higher.

Need pounded through her veins, need for more, need for Rand. She melted against him, holding him, swaying with him as his hips pumped in an erotic rhythm.

He groaned and enfolded her tightly, pressing her to him, filling one hand with a hank of hair and tilting her head farther back. His mouth plundered hers, and she welcomed it, took the thrust of his tongue and returned it, answered her body's desire to surge against his from knee to breast, to accede to every demand.

The thin knit fabric of her leggings was no shield against the heat of his skin, the rasp of the hair on his thigh. The delicious sensations forced her legs farther apart as she sought the rough texture of him against her inner thighs, the hardness of his arousal against the moist heat of her own. She grew heavy, dizzy, her head swirling, and the sounds they both made coming from far, far away.

This wasn't enough. She needed more, so much more. She could fight it no longer, fight herself no longer. With a soft, inarticulate cry, she surrendered to her need.

NINE

As Kat's warm, yielding body slumped heavily against him, Rand caught her up in his arms. Turning, he took two staggering strides until he reached the sofa. He laid her down and followed before his own knees gave way, stretching out beside her.

"Kat . . . Ah, baby," he murmured as he slid a hand over her body, pausing at her breasts, moving down over her belly, pressing the palm of his hand between her legs. They fell apart at his touch as if she'd been dying for it, and he stroked her, feeling her heat, loving it, wanting it to surround him, ease him, please him.

But not yet. He couldn't rush, wouldn't. It had been too long for him to hurry this delight. He owed her so much, wanted to give her so much, show her what she was to him. His wife, yes, but his lover, his precious, adored lover.

He bent and took her mouth again, his tongue plunging as he wanted to plunge into her. Her hips moved instinctively to the same rhythm as his bold, explicit caresses. "Yes, babe," he gasped, lifting his head for a moment. He felt her deep shudders of pleasure, felt his own need build and strengthen until he knew he was in danger of bursting with it. "That's right. It's good, isn't it?"

She made a soft sound of assent, lifting her hips as her legs spread wider to admit his stroking hand. Her ragged breathing, the deep tremors shuddering through her supple body, alerted him, and he slowed his caresses, not wanting to let her rush either. He moved his hand up to the front of her sweater, undid several buttons, and bent his head to kiss the upper curves of her breasts.

Feeling her shiver, he ran his tongue along the outline of her bra cups, tasting her skin, savoring her. She held his head in her hands, caressing his hair, his ears, his cheeks. He heard the rasp of her palms on his whiskers, and lifted his head to look at her. A red rash was already forming around her mouth, on her throat, on the pale, blue-veined curves of her breasts.

He groaned and rubbed his prickly jaw. "Oh, hell, honey, I'm sorry!" He touched the rash gently with his fingertips. "Look what I've done to you."

Kat forgot that her eyes were bloodshot, forgot that her face was ugly and blotchy from crying. She cupped his face in her hands and lifted her head to kiss him. "Oh, no," she said against his lips. "Don't stop. Please, Rand. Kiss me again. It doesn't hurt."

His mouth twisted. "It hurts me, Kat. Oh, God, how it hurts me to know I've hurt you."

She looked at him, saw the passion, the need, the hunger in his face. Wrapping her hands around his neck, she pulled him down to her, her need as great as his, her hunger as intense. "If this is pain, then I'm a masochist."

He laughed softly and touched her lips with his.

"Rand, please!" she said when he lifted his head after the briefest of kisses. "Not having you hurts me more." She closed her eyes, her head tossing from side to side. "Oh, please . . ." she whispered.

"Please, what?" He cupped her breast, massaging it gently through thin satin. "This?" He unfastened her bra, pulled it away, and tasted the special tang of a nipple, kissing it, sucking it into his mouth. She sighed, moving from side to side as he curved his palm around the other breast, thumbnail stroking over its tip. "Beautiful," he breathed.

"They've shrunk." She wished she could hide them with her hands. As her husband, he'd delighted in her breasts, but never more than when she was pregnant or nursing.

"They're smaller," he said, "but I love them just the same."

"I went off the pill. Rand . . . oh, Lord, but that feels good."

"Better than this?" He slid his callused hand down over her bare stomach. It quivered and jumped at his touch.

"No. Yes . . . I . . ." Her words became an inarticulate moan as she arched to him and he caressed her damp heat again, pressing his palm against her mound, his fingers moving between her legs. She rocked against him, running her hand down his front, capturing his erection in her fist and eliciting a groan of pleasure.

He bent his leg, and she raked her nails along his thigh, from knee to edge of ragged denim and back again. "Touch me!" His voice was curt, harsh, urgent. He shifted to one side, providing more access. Her fingers curved over him again, nails rasping on denim. "Undo my pants, Kat. Touch me."

"I'm trying, I'm trying," she said, fighting with the snap at the top of his shorts, their mutual impatience impeding her. Nothing mattered but doing what he wanted, what she *needed*. As she fought with his zipper, he took her breast into his mouth, sucking hard, deep. Her womb contracted in almost painful spasms.

She won her struggle with his shorts and slid her hand inside, slipped past the elastic waistband of his underwear and onto the heat of his skin. As her hand closed around his distended flesh, they both became very still, gazes locked, mouths half-parted, then a shudder ran through him. His head fell back against the cushions. A long, growling sound arose from his throat.

Without loosening her grip, Kat moved her hand, an inch up, an inch down. The silky heat of him was exactly as she remembered. The hard strength of him throbbing in her palm, the scent rising from his hot body, was as heady. It melted her, scalded her, made her tremble all over with need. She stroked him again, longer, stronger, dragging another moan from his throat.

"God, I want you!" he said, tearing her hand off him and fumbling for the elastic waist of her leggings. "Now, babe. Right now!" She lifted her hips, knowing what was to come, welcoming it, needing it, needing him.

"Yes," she said, her voice all but lost in the shrill sound ringing in her head. She fought to ignore it, saying again, "Oh, yes . . . Oh, Rand . . . Oh, *damn!* Rand, stop!"

She caught his hands, stilling them against her hips with her leggings half-down.

"Stop," she repeated.

"What?" He lifted his head, his face white, his eyes burning. "Stop? Why?" Sweat beaded on his upper lip, catching in the dark beard stubble.

"The phone . . ." It rang again. "It might be one of the kids."

"No . . ." He couldn't believe this. "No!"

She struggled to get free. "They might need me. Rand, I can't neglect the kids!"

He stared at her. Kids? he wanted to say. What kids? But he knew what kids and knew she was right. He groaned and levered himself upward, leaned over, and picked up the shrilling phone.

"Yes?" he barked, then he nodded and said, "Kate? Kate who? Oh. Yeah. Sure. Just a minute. Here she is."

"It's for you," he said thrusting the phone at her. He got to his feet and did up his shorts, glaring at her as she fumbled the phone. She dropped it onto her lap and tangled the cord around her wrist as she tried to control her shaking hands.

"Your boyfriend, I guess," he added, his voice cold, his eyes like twin bits of blackened steel. "One of them." He turned and strode from the room without looking back.

"Craig," Kat said when she finally lifted the phone. Her throat was so tight, she could scarcely force speech out. Only two people in the world ever called her Kate. Craig and his mother. "What do you want?"

"For starters," he said, "I want to know who that man was."

"Rand," she said, hearing the back door slam. "Rand . . ."

She wasn't sure if she was answering Craig's question or simply saying Rand's name, wishing he'd come back. If he had, she'd have dropped the phone and returned to his arms. She burned. She ached. Her whole body continued to pulse with need for his lovemaking.

"Rand?" Craig's shock was evident. "As in Randall Waddell, your husband?"

"Yes." Outside, the lawn mower started, a high, angry whine. Kat pinned the phone between shoulder and chin as she did up her bra. "Ex-husband."

Oh, Lord! What had she done?

"Kate, don't quibble."

"Don't call me Kate," she said automatically, starting on the buttons of her sweater. He only called her that because his mother thought "Kat" was a silly name for a grown woman.

What she'd done was almost make love with her ex-husband.

"Katherine, what is your ex-husband doing at your house?"

Turning me inside out.

"I believe he's mowing the lawn."

"Mowing the— What in the world for?"

She stood and adjusted the top of her leggings around her waist, then walked as close to the window as the phone cord permitted. Rand strode down the backyard, racing with the mower, grass flying from its side. He hadn't put the bag on. "I suppose he's mowing it because the grass is too long," she said, her mind only half on Craig. *He's mowing it because he's in a foul temper.*

Rand looked very, very angry. Or very, very frustrated. Or both. A small sound of distress escaped her.

"Kate, what is wrong?"

"Nothing . . ." Oh, Lord, she was crying, sobbing aloud the way Katie did when her heart was broken.

"That does it," Craig said. "You're acting much too strange. I'm coming over there."

"Craig! No!" She managed to choke back her hysterical weeping. She didn't want to see Craig today. She thought she probably would never want to see Craig again, though that was unfair and illogical. He'd been a good friend and had had utterly no way of knowing what his call might interrupt. "Don't do that. Please. There's no need. I'm all right now."

"My dear Kate, there is every need! Clearly, you're not 'all right,' nor are you thinking straight. Don't you know how it could prejudice your entire case, letting that man do yard maintenance?"

Kat shook her head. She must have missed something, somewhere. "Case?" She really, really hated it when Craig pulled his lawyer stuff on her. She blew her nose hard.

"When you need more money from him," he said with grave patience, as if she were a child of limited intelligence. "It won't do you any good if he can prove to the court that he's had a hand in maintaining the house where you and the children live."

"It's his house too."

"Technically, maybe. But you live there, Kat. He doesn't."

She drew a deep breath and let it out slowly. "As a matter of fact, Craig, he does."

The resulting explosion was very satisfying, as well

as edifying. She hadn't realized just how badly Craig had misconstrued their friendship or her intentions toward him. She'd thought by refusing to go to that contest in Seattle with him and share a hotel room, she'd made it clear. Obviously, she had not. Now, she made sure she did, politely at first, then when he argued, much more forcefully.

She hung up with a vengeance almost simultaneously with Craig.

Outside, Rand still charged back and forth, up and down the lawn.

She stood at the window and glared out at him. His chest and shoulders glistened with sweat in the sunlight. Moisture beaded on his forehead and poured down his face. Her emotions still running high from her argument with Craig, she stomped outside and pulled the plug on the mower. Rand whirled to face her. His anger was clearly stronger than his frustration.

"What the hell did you do that for?"

"I don't want you having a heart attack in my backyard."

"I'll have a heart attack anywhere I damned well please," he snarled, and snatched the cord away from her, yanking it back toward him. It danced across the yard like a demented snake. "Go and chat with your boyfriend some more. I don't need you out here."

"Just leave my lawn alone. I don't need *you* any-where!"

"That's not the way I remember it," he said, his eyes narrow, his mouth taut. "Want to return to the family-room couch, Katherine?"

"Never!"

He grabbed up the plug and rammed it into an

outlet in the toolshed, then flung a pair of words at her. Over the renewed noise of the mower, she didn't hear them, but she could read his lips just fine.

She gaped at him. He had *never* said anything like that to her, not even when their marriage was at its very worst. She wished she had a shovel in her hand so she could knock his block off. Maybe he was where Nathan had learned that word. Nathan's mouth she could wash with soap. Mrs. Perfect Mother should have done the same to her little boy thirty years ago.

As he strode away, she glared at him until her eyes burned from lack of blinking. He turned at the end of the yard and marched back toward her. His jaw was set in a square block of determination. He looked like a man who had sworn death to grass.

What the hell did he have to be so angry about? He had no right to expect her not to have friends, no call to throw a tantrum because one of them accidentally interrupted a necking session that should never have happened in the first place.

And he had no right to use gutter language on her! Eagerly, gratefully, she let anger boil up until it filled her, destroying any vestige of any other roiling emotion that might have remained.

Anger was good. It was clean. It was something she could understand.

Her hands itched for something to do. Her legs twitched with the need to move. Her arms hummed with power that had no outlet. Dammit, wasn't that her lawn he was taking out his frustrations on? Wasn't she entitled to a few of those herself and a way to vent them? What she should do is wrestle that damned mower away from him, demand that he let her do the job. But if she did, he'd tell her to go scrub a toilet, as a good little woman should.

Hah! If the house weren't so squeaky-clean, she probably would. With another burning, furious glare at her ex-husband, who returned it in kind, she watched as Rand strode around the side of the house, heading for the front yard.

All right then. She'd let him have the physical release of cutting the grass. It was a job she hated, anyway. It was right up there with cleaning toilets on her list of loathsome chores.

She would rake.

As she snatched the rake out of the storage shed and began dragging it through the cut grass, she ground her teeth together. What in the hell had come over the two of them? It must have been some kind of craziness. Whatever it was, she was damned if she'd ever let it happen again.

With fury to speed her, she had the back lawn raked in no time. When Rand returned with the mower from the front, she left her pile of grass cuttings and stomped around to rake where he'd been.

When that was done, and the grass all picked up and disposed of, there was no sign of him. She was glad, glad, glad! Maybe he'd gone out. Maybe he'd fallen down a hole. Maybe an alien spaceship had scooped him up and carried him away to an eternity of slavery, making crop circles with her lawn mower.

She stomped inside, not bothering to ask herself why her irritation with Craig, with herself, with a situation she had helped create, had become so focused on Rand.

She had showered for the third time that day and

dressed again when Katie phoned asking permission to eat at Parjeet's house. She gave it gladly. She was in no frame of mind to be civil to anyone, not even her little daughter.

In the kitchen ten minutes later she stood staring into the fridge, considering what she could put in a sandwich for supper, or whether she should bother with supper at all.

Rand knocked on the door leading from the laundry room to the kitchen.

She wrenched it open. "What?" she said, a woman who had taken all she meant to take that day.

His easy smile did nothing to lessen her annoyance. He had shaved, showered, and dressed in a pale green shirt that was almost an exact match for the tracksuit she wore. That raised her hackles, too, most irration-ally. "Hey," he said. "Let's not be mad anymore."

She blinked. "What?"

"Same word, different intonation. I guess that's progress." His smile fading, he went on. "Kat, I acted like a jerk today after that phone call. I'm trying to apologize. Okay?"

She couldn't speak for a minute. "When a jerk mows my lawn, even if he does it because he's in a temper, I guess I have to accept his apology."

He leaned in the doorway. His gaze seemed to caress her face. A slow, insidious warmth, not entirely sexual, began to rise inside her. "I was a jerk, too, and I apologize," she said. It amazed her to discover how easy it was to do that.

Before, both she and Rand would have eaten live slugs rather than apologize to each other. Usually, fights were simply let to fade into the past, never discussed. It was as if they'd decided early on that if they didn't pay attention to their differences, they could pretend they didn't exist.

How wrong they had been.

"Where are the kids?" he asked after a moment.

"Still where they were the last time you asked."

His right eyebrow raised in query, either at her manner or her judgment as a mother. "Isn't it almost dinnertime?" he asked mildly. "Would you like me to go and get Katie?"

Maybe he hadn't been questioning her judgment as a mother this time. Maybe she should give him the benefit of the doubt. She shook her head. "She's eating dinner with her friend. Nathan's birthday party is scheduled to end up at McDonald's. He'll be home at seven-thirty. I told Katie I'd come and walk her home just before then."

He looked at her for several moments, then asked softly, "And you, Kat? Do you have any plans for the next two hours?"

She thought of the sandwich she intended to make. Lifting her chin an inch, she opened her mouth to say yes and heard a soft, wistful voice say, "No. None at all."

"Good," he said. "How does a hamburger sound? Triple O and all the trimmings."

She closed her eyes for a second and jammed her suddenly shaking hands into the big patch pockets on the front of her sweatshirt. An image popped into her mind: The second time they'd met, it had been over a hamburger at one of the few remaining drive-in restaurants in the area.

She'd loved the thick, gooshy hamburgers with what

the owners called "triple O" sauce, but never more than when Rand had leaned over and used his thumb to wipe a dribble of it off her chin. Then, with a harsh intake of breath, he'd shoved the tray out of the way, cupped her face in his hands and licked the sauce from her lips. That had led to a deep, heated kiss that had left them both dazed and shaken. He'd alternated feeding her bites of her burger with kissing her, until their meal was finished and their bodies both cried out for release.

They'd almost made love that night in his car, in a park overlooking the city, but a cruising cop had shone his spotlight on them. Reluctantly, Rand had taken her back to the YWCA where she had a room.

The next weekend, three days later, they'd gone away together. . . .

"Kat?" His voice was soft, beguiling.

She sighed and capitulated. "You know all the right buttons to push, don't you, Waddell?"

"I hope so, babe." He punched her lightly on the chin, and she saw in his eyes a serious expression that didn't quite match his easy tone. "Because I aim to push them, one right after another, until you're playing a tune we both can dance to."

He took her hand, and they were halfway out to his car before she remembered to breathe. And before she remembered that Rand had stopped dancing with her a long, long time ago.

If he really intended to start again, she wasn't sure she remembered the steps.

He bowed her into the passenger seat with a sweep of his arm, all gentlemanly and suave and grinning as he showed off for her. When he was behind the wheel, though, his grin faded. He turned to her, took her hand again, and smoothed his thumb over the bare spot where her rings should have been.

"We started something today, Kat," he said. "I'd like to see us continue it."

She pulled her hand free as alarm warred with heat—this time totally sexual—inside her. "I don't think so. It's a bad, bad idea. Remember what I said the day you asked if you could come move into the suite? Today was the same thing, I think. We'd been talking about Jen and Karl, remembering, grieving. And then our bodies wanted to . . . celebrate life."

He smiled. "It was a wonderful celebration, Kat."

His eyes dared her to deny it. She couldn't. "It was wonderful," she agreed. She swallowed hard before she could go on. "But it wouldn't be wonderful for long. We just aren't good for each other. We have too many problems, Rand, too many differences, simply to kiss and make up."

"Yeah." He stared at his hands on the steering wheel. "But maybe we could work on those problems, those differences. Actually, that's what I was talking about when I said we'd made a start that I'd like us to continue. Talking, Kitty-Kat. Communicating, as the experts like to call it."

She bit her lip. "I don't know. Every time we try to talk, we end up fighting again."

He met her gaze, held it, as they both remembered the ugly scenes, the cruel words they'd exchanged in the past. "But . . . there's a difference now. Don't you see it? Don't you feel it? When we talk, we seem to be saying different things from what we said before. And when we fight, we both hold back a bit."

She chewed on her bottom lip. He was right. She

remembered several times over the past few weeks when she'd been about to cut loose with something scathing and had bitten her tongue. If he was willing to do the same, then maybe . . .

"I think we can make it work, talking together, Katherine."

She sighed. She really, really liked it when he called her Katherine with no vexation in his voice. It was as if he had somehow begun to see her as a mature adult who deserved an adult name.

She moved restlessly in her seat, did up her safety belt, undid it again. "Before, when I wanted us to talk about our problems, you usually walked away." She clicked her belt shut. "Or we yelled at each other." And opened it again.

He jammed the end of her seat belt into its clasp and held a hand over it so she couldn't undo it again. "I know," he said. "It scared me, knowing we had problems. I guess I sort of put you into a little box labeled 'Wife and Mother.' When you wanted to put another label on it, maybe push out the sides of it to give yourself more room, I tried too hard to shove the walls of it back in on you.

"I was wrong. I know that now. I told you, I've changed."

Doubts churned inside her, battling a hint of hope.

"Kat . . ." He took her hand, held it loosely in his. "Katherine, if you could talk to Jenny—about me— what would you say?"

She couldn't look at him. She could scarcely breathe. "I guess that I'm . . . confused. That when I look at you, today, I see a whole lot of the man I fell in love with, the man I married."

But I don't see so much of the man I almost came to hate.

She wished she could say that, but the words stuck in her throat. "Then—then I look again," she went on finally, "and I see a completely different man. A stranger I don't know anymore."

"So you're agreeing I've changed?" His voice was a soft rumble, settling around her, easing her heart.

She nodded, lifting her gaze to his face. "But I don't know how to react to those changes. I don't know how . . . genuine they are. Or how permanent."

"Okay. I can understand that. Will you give me a chance to show you? I put myself into a little box, too, Katherine. And as I changed, I guess I grew until the mold I thought I fit into broke."

He put the car in gear and backed out of the driveway. Kat looked over her shoulder automatically to be sure the way was clear.

He laughed shortly. "That used to irritate the hell out of me, you know. Your looking over your shoulder when I'm in the driver's seat."

Guiltily, she whipped her head around. "I'm sorry. It's no reflection on your driving abilities. It's just, I guess, that I think two sets of eyes are better than one."

"And that two incomes are better than one."

"I still think that, Rand, but it was more than an income I wanted. It was a sense of self-worth that staying home never gave me. Besides, I was lonely with you away so much. Lonely for adult companionship."

At the corner he braked to a stop. "You had Jenny."

With great effort Kat kept her gaze straight ahead

while Rand checked for oncoming traffic. "True," she said. "But Jenny and Karl had a life, too, you know. I couldn't live in their pockets."

The car rolled forward. Very quietly, Rand said, "I know that. I knew it at the time. I managed to go on believing for a long time that I needed to be sole provider to prove myself worthy as a man, but there was more to it than that."

"What more was there?" she asked when he'd driven several blocks without saying anything else.

"I, um, didn't want you working where there were men."

She stared at his set profile. "*You* didn't trust *me*?"

He shrugged and shot her a quick glance. "You didn't trust me, Kat."

She couldn't deny it. Any more than he had ever denied that she'd had good reason to distrust him.

"I never broke my vows," she said, then almost held her breath, wondering if he would say the same. If she'd really been hoping for it, she'd have been disappointed. What did she want, for him to lie to her as her father had lied to her mother? Would she be better able to believe a lie—had he cared enough to fabricate one—now than she had been then?

"I know," he said. "I knew it back then, too, but I was afraid you might. That you'd be tempted. I was jealous. Insecure."

She drew a deep breath. He'd always seemed the most self-confident person to her. The idea of his being insecure was almost ludicrous. Almost. Except, it did explain an awful lot. "Why?" she asked.

"Because . . ." He let that trail off with an exasperated sigh. "How the hell do I know? I just was. The way you just were. Because neither of us ever learned to trust other people very much, I guess. Right now, I only wish you'd trust the changes you admit to seeing in me. Trust me enough to accept me back into your life . . . in one way or another."

Still, she hesitated. "No pressure," he said. "No sex if you're not ready for that kind of commitment. Just talking. Being together. Maybe doing the courting we didn't take time for the first time around. Or, if you prefer, nothing more than friendship."

At length she nodded. "Okay. It's a deal." She didn't say what was a deal, though. Rand, to her surprise, didn't press to learn what it was she'd agreed to. Which was lucky. What was it she wanted from him, with him? Talk? Friendship? Courting? Something quivered inside her at the thought of a courtship.

He took her left hand in his right, because it was the one he could reach, and solemnly, awkwardly, shook it. "It's a better deal than I've had in a long, long time, Ms. Waddell."

She smiled. "Me, too, Mr. Waddell. Me too."

TEN

It was the most pleasant meal they had shared in years, Kat reflected as they drove home—despite their having eaten their gooshy hamburgers inside the restaurant rather than in the car and having used napkins to wipe their mouths. Every once in a while she'd see a trickle of sauce on Rand's lips, and a stab of heat sliced through her. Every now and then she noticed his gaze on her mouth, hot and disturbing, and she knew that he, too, remembered. Neither spoke of those memories. Oddly, that made them all the more potent for Kat.

Later, as they walked along the block to fetch Katie home, Rand took her hand and drew her to a halt under a tree just outside what had been Jenny and Karl's home.

"Who lives there now?" he asked.

She tried to keep walking, but he held her at his side, looking at the house Kat was always careful to keep her eyes averted from.

"An older couple," she said. "They're very nice."

"Any kids?"

"A teenaged daughter who sometimes baby-sits for me, and an older one in college."

"Do you visit with them?"

"No." She shook her head. "Rand, let's go. It's time Katie was home."

"Have you been in that house since . . . ?"

"Yes," she said impatiently. "Once or twice." It had seemed almost like a desecration, seeing someone else's furniture in Jenny's house, someone else's car in the drive, different paint on the outside. She had gone to welcome the new neighbors, hoping that seeing the changes they had made might make the memory of her last visit with Jenny fade from the horrible sharpness it retained.

It had not.

"We argued," she said. "Jenny and I. The day they were packing to go to Karl's parents' for Christmas." A wafting breeze shook the tree overhead, sending a shower of cherry blossoms onto them. "I stomped out of her house, mad. And I never got to tell her I was sorry."

"Ah, honey," he said, brushing a handful of fallen pink petals off her hair. "Jen knew that. And I bet she wished she could have told you she was sorry too."

Kat looked at him in the dusk. "I don't know. She was really mad at me." He curved his hand around her jaw, fingers sliding into her hair. She flinched. "Rand," she said. "Please don't."

"What were you and Jenny arguing about?" he asked.

"I, um, just . . . stuff."

Rand heard the note of desperation in her tone. He knew he should back off, but he had to know. "It was about us, wasn't it?"

She closed her eyes. "Yes," she said softly, then looked at him. "Us." Her voice cracked on the word. He drew her against his chest, meaning to hold her again for just a moment. "She blamed me for not inviting you to share Christmas with u—with the kids."

Rand clenched his teeth as he stroked a taut hand through her silky tresses. That had been his fault. He'd let Jen see how down he was, because it was Christmas, and he had to spend it without the kids that year. Without the kids and Kat. The year before, he'd had Katie and Nathan, and Kat had gone to Jenny and Karl's for the day.

"She reminded me," Kat went on, "of how blue I'd been the year before, and told me off for not asking you." She shook off his hand and looked up at him. "Would you have come?"

He thought about it. "I don't know. I really don't."

"I told her I was sure you wouldn't. But that wasn't my reason for not asking. I was . . . afraid to see you. Afraid to face up to the mess we'd made of things."

He hugged her tightly. "Messes can be cleaned up, Katherine."

She slipped free. "Not this one, Rand."

"Don't bet the farm, babe. I think we've made a damned good start already. Aren't we friends?"

"Sure," she said. "We're friends." At least they had learned they could apologize without losing ground.

And maybe "friends" wasn't such a bad place to start.

❦―――――❦

"Friends," Todd said, "tell each other what's eating them, Kat. You've moped all afternoon, hardly said a word. Your enthusiasm over Redmond's triple play would have made an undertaker look cheerful. What's up? Is it that husband of yours?"

"He's not my husband. I just miss the kids. I never feel good when they're gone. You know that."

"Yeah, but you never used to brood the way you do now when he takes them away. You used to enjoy your free weekends."

"Yes, but this is the second weekend in a row the three of them have gone camping. I know we agreed not to be formal about our weekends, but it hardly seems fair for him to have done that. He's with them more than I am now." Rand had also invited her along, pointing out that there was more than enough room in the motor home he'd rented. She'd strongly resisted temptation and declined.

"If you didn't like it," Todd said, "you could have said so."

Kat looked askance. "The kids wanted to go. I can't deprive them of fun just because I miss them."

"I think," Todd said, tilting his baseball cap back, "it's Rand you miss as much, and maybe even more, than the kids."

She crumpled her mustard-spotted paper napkin and tossed it into a garbage can at the edge of the parking lot. "That's ridiculous."

"Is it?" he asked, opening the passenger door of his Jeep. "I don't think so."

Kat said nothing as she climbed in. There was nothing she could say. How could she refute his argument when she wasn't certain he was wrong?

Todd sat behind the wheel and watched traffic crawl out of the lot as other fans, in more of a hurry than he, left.

"I'm going to stop coming around," he said finally. "I don't think we should see each other anymore."

"No!" she protested. "Todd, why?"

"Because I think it's time for you to get a life, Kat," he said, finally slotting the Jeep into a gap between cars. "One that includes that husband of yours. You're in love with him. You want him? Go for it. Don't wait for him to come to you. Guys are scared to do that nowadays."

"Rand?" she hooted. "Rand's not scared of anything."

Kat might have laughed then, but over the next few days Todd's words kept returning to haunt her.

The first time was when she came home from work and found Rand had dug up two strips of lawn along the sides of the driveway. He'd had truckloads of topsoil brought in, and as she arrived, he was planting the last of what must have been a shocking dollar value in pansies. Picking one, he walked over to her car as she opened the door.

He handed the flower to her, his gaze on her face. "For you, my lady. I wish it could be a dozen red roses, but they aren't in bloom yet."

Stunned and incredibly moved by the romantic gesture, she took the little flower, stroking its velvety purple petals over her cheek. "Thank you, Rand."

She'd meant it to be a bright, friendly phrase, but it came out as a small, broken whisper. Blinking rapidly, she stared down at the pansy. She knew he'd only done it because of what she'd said about his being unromantic, but for all that, it touched something tender inside her.

"Hey," he said, "you can't cry! I did this for you. I wanted to make you happy."

She swallowed hard. "I know. And I am. Very happy." She looked at the single pansy she held, then gazed out over the massed colors of the border. "It's very beautiful, and I can see how hard you must have worked. Thank you."

He leaned his hip on the hood of her car and slid a hand around her waist. "Is that all I get?" he asked suggestively.

Kat's heart took off. She glanced around. "Where are Nathan and Katie?"

He grinned. "Out back playing in a load of bark mulch I got. So we're all alone."

"Oh," she said. They were far from being alone. There were neighbors in view all along the block, working in gardens, cutting lawns, strolling. Children played, riding bikes, Rollerblades, skateboards. But did neighbors really matter?

No. Not as much as this. She slid one hand behind his head, drew his face down, and kissed his lips. He didn't move, merely accepted what she offered, but as she stepped back, she saw how much she'd pleased him. "There," she said, feeling a bubble of happiness well up inside. "Satisfied?"

He laughed aloud and hugged her tightly, lifting her off the ground. "Not by a long shot. But I'll take what I can get. For now."

That night seemed to set a pattern. She'd come

home, and if the weather was nice, she'd find him outside in the garden, sometimes with the kids around, other times not. When that happened, he normally found a valid reason for her to kiss him, or for him to kiss her. She came to expect it, to look forward to it, to speculate during the day on what excuse he'd find to brush his lips over hers, to pull her close and hold her for a moment.

The day after he saw her examining the fat buds on her lilac bush and heard her encouraging it to bloom for the first time in its life, he welcomed her home with a huge bouquet of dark purple lilacs in the living room. "A nice lady in the next block gave them to me," he said. "I stopped and asked her why hers were blooming and ours isn't. She says it's because hers is an old, established bush and is planted right next to her house where it's sheltered. Maybe we should move ours?"

More and more, Kat liked to hear pronouns like "ours" and "we."

But it was the night she and Rand danced together that made her realize Todd had been absolutely right. She was in love with Rand.

That night, the Saturday of a weekend he'd told the kids they weren't going anywhere because their mom deserved some time with them, too, he came to tuck them in as usual. Then, as had also become customary, he sat with Kat, and they chatted for a while.

The difference came when he stood and reached for her hand. "Think they're sound asleep now?" he asked.

"I imagine so. Why?"

"Because I have something for you. Downstairs."

"Really?" She let him pull her to her feet. "What?"

"A surprise. Come and see."

He had cleaned out the basement, restoring an order that it hadn't seen for years. Junk, leftover furniture, boxes—their contents unknown—had been stacked against walls, leaving a wide expanse of clear floor. That, he'd obviously washed, because the gray paint on the concrete fairly gleamed.

"Rand! So that's what you were doing all afternoon. I thought you were drawing." She'd felt hurt that on this one weekend he'd deigned to spend at home, he'd left her to garden all alone. He did it ostensibly to give her time with the kids, both of whom had played all day with their friends. "Thank you," she said. "The basement has needed a good cleaning for a long time."

"Ah, but that's not why I did it. Hold on to me now," he ordered, and reached for the switch that controlled the bright, fluorescent lighting. The cavernous room went instantly dark. "Now, come with me," he said. Intrigued, she followed, sliding her feet gingerly though she knew there were no obstacles in her path. He reached the side of the basement and opened the door to his suite, then reached in and flipped another switch.

Soft light flooded the basement from lamps he'd placed around the walls, and along with the glow came strains of music. Kat saw that he'd brought his speakers out of the suite and positioned them at opposite ends of the room.

She stood still and listened to the sweet notes of the music, fighting back an ache in her throat. It was one of the pieces they had once loved to dance to.

"Oh, Rand . . ." She met his gaze and saw the intensity in his eyes, the myriad questions.

"I haven't heard your music for a couple of weeks," he said. "I thought maybe you missed dancing."

She nodded. "I do."

"Where is he?" Rand asked, his voice taut. "Your friend, the one you danced with?"

"We agreed to disagree. So I guess I'm out a dancing partner."

Rand shook his head. "Maybe not." He laughed self-consciously when his voice cracked a little. "Ms. Waddell," he went on more firmly, but she saw that his hand shook slightly as he held it out to her, palm up. "May I have this dance, please?"

Kat trembled as she swayed into his arms and felt them close around her. They made one full circuit of the floor without speaking. They made another, and he shifted his hand on her back, sliding it down to the flare of her hip. His hand was hot through her clothes.

Their steps were perfectly matched. She sensed his intentions and moved with him instinctively. It had always been this way. He turned her, dipped her, looked into her eyes, and smiled his satisfaction.

"Beautiful," he said.

She leaned back against his arm. "I'm not dressed for this." She regretted her jeans and T-shirt. Always before, when they had danced in their unfurnished living room, she had dressed up for it. It had been part of the ritual, part of the fun. "I should have on a swirly skirt."

"I can see your skirt," he said, spinning her across the floor. "It's bright blue and has white flowers on it.

And when I do this"—he whirled her into a dizzying spin—"it swirls out all around you."

She laughed. Did he really remember that cotton skirt she'd had when they first got married? "How long is it?" she challenged him.

"When we're dancing close, like this"—he swept her tightly against his body—"it's just about knee-length. But when I do this"—he spun her away from him again, twirling her around and around with her hand over her head—"it flares out and shows me your thighs right up to the lace of your panties.

"They," he whispered, drawing her into his arms again, "are bright red, and the lace is black. They are incredibly sexy, and I want to look and look."

His words sent a hot shaft of desire through her, and she shuddered as if he had really just looked at her panties and found them "incredibly sexy."

They danced until they were breathless, until they were parched, then Rand opened beers for them. They sat on the edge of a stack of lumber left over from years gone by. Kat wondered when he would start seducing her with kisses that she knew she'd be powerless to resist, wondered when he would try to draw her into his suite, his bed. . . .

She wondered, too, if she would be able to resist that.

She didn't have to make that kind of choice, though. When they were rested, they danced again, until she had to call a halt.

"Yeah, me too," he said, running a hand through his damp hair and leaving it sticking up all over. "The body's not used to that kind of exercise. Time for bed."

He slid his arm around her, walked her to the kitchen door, and brushed a hot kiss over her lips.

"Thank you," he said. "That was the best evening I've spent in a long, long time." He stroked her cheek with one finger. "Think we can do it again sometime?"

Kat couldn't speak. She could only nod her head.

"Good," he said. "We'll make it soon."

He turned and went back downstairs, leaving Kat to trail off to bed alone.

Which brought her back to what Todd had said. If a move was to be made to change their relationship, to advance it, was it indeed up to her to make it?

She wanted to. And she certainly knew how to. The night had not had to end this way. She could, at any time, have changed the pattern of things. Why hadn't she?

Over the weeks he'd spent back in the house, she had seen how drastically Rand had changed. If it hadn't been for the counseling he'd admitted having taken, she'd be less willing to believe those changes could be real, or that they might be lasting.

If she hadn't witnessed with her own eyes his new attitudes, his depth of understanding, not only of her and her needs but of himself and what governed his actions, she'd have doubted that he was capable of that degree of growth.

And she, too, had changed. She, too, had grown. As had their relationship. Yes, they still argued. Sometimes they even fought. But there was a distinct difference, she thought. Neither of them was out to wound the other, as they had once been. They both held back; and she had already acknowledged that it was easier for them to apologize now. That had to be seen as progress, but was it enough?

What if . . . Kat rolled over in her bed, trying to quell the thought, trying to choke back the sick feeling those memories always gave her. Still, the feeling, and the memories, rushed up. What if Rand were to apologize for *that*? What if he were to ask her forgiveness for what she had once seen as unforgivable?

Could she forgive?

She might be able to love Rand. She might be able to take him back. But how could she ever trust him again? Would she wonder, each time they were apart, if he was with another woman? Would she let it haunt her as she had in the months when they had been estranged before she left him? Would the constant doubt sour any new relationship they might form?

She knew that other women had managed to forgive infidelity. She wondered, though, if they had ever been able, really, to forget.

If she and Rand were to have a chance, she knew she'd have to find some way to do both.

"Come for dinner," Rand said a few days later. To Kat's surprise, it was easy to smile and agree. It was not so easy to hide her eagerness.

She sat in stunned awe at the meal he prepared and the evident enjoyment he took in cooking. As if roast beef, crispy roast potatoes, Yorkshire pudding, and two vegetables weren't enough, he produced a moist dark chocolate cake with thick, luscious icing for dessert. She ate every crumb and licked her fingers.

"Come on, confess," she said, after he had excused

the kids so they could watch TV in the living room of his suite. He poured coffee for himself and Kat, and they stayed at the galley table by tacit mutual consent. "You sneaked out to a deli and bought all this."

He laughed. "I confess no such thing. I slaved over a hot stove all afternoon." Sobering, he took her hand and slipped it under the table with his. "I told you, Kat, I've changed."

She let her fingers lie curled within his. "Yes," she said. "I know you have." She smiled as she thought about the night they had danced together. The old Rand would have relied on seduction to get what he wanted. It was a measure of his new maturity that he had not. "When did you discover that you liked cooking?"

He grinned. "When I got tired of peanut-butter sandwiches, I took a course in the basics. The instructor said I was a natural and gave me extra lessons at home when the course was over, so I could learn a bit more. We're still good friends."

She felt her body tense but forced herself to continue looking into his eyes. "She was right," she said. "You are a natural."

"He was right," he said, stressing the pronoun. "We do lots of things together, Joe and I. I want you to meet him and his wife. I thought about inviting them tonight, but this place is too small for entertaining."

Kat's smile felt tenuous. Her "Oh" was a breathy whisper. Clearing her throat, she said, "Maybe sometime we—you could invite them and use the dining room upstairs."

Rand's fingers tightened a fraction. "Maybe sometime we will."

They both fell silent, listening to the sounds from the living room. The TV. Their children giggling. Then, speaking quietly, he said, "Kat, there haven't been any women."

She stared at him until her eyes burned, then dropped her gaze. "I'm sorry."

He tilted her face up. "Why? Because there have been men for you? We're divorced, Kat. You had every right."

She could have told him that dating was all she'd done with both Craig and Todd, but she didn't. She wasn't ready to make confessions of that nature to him. She didn't know what he might read into it, or what conclusions she wanted him to draw—if any.

"That's not what I meant," she said. "I'm sorry if you've been . . . lonely. I know what it's like out there. Dangerous."

"I know how to practice safe sex if I have to," he said quietly. "But like I said a while back, I simply wasn't in the mood." He gave her a crooked grin. "That's something I have in common with most of the men from my discussion group. It seems a newly separated man either turns into a baboon or becomes an introvert."

"And you became an introvert."

He nodded. "There's something else I want you to know." He stirred his coffee, tapped the spoon on the edge of his cup, then set it down carefully before he looked at her again. "I never had another woman. After we got married. There was no affair."

She stared at him, not believing, remembering the anguish.

She'd had pneumonia, been so sick she couldn't

cope. She'd called the paper to ask to have Rand brought home from wherever they'd sent him. They'd said there must be a mistake, that he wasn't on assignment but on vacation. He'd taken emergency personal leave.

"No affair?" she asked.

He looked deep into her eyes. "No affair. Not even a one-night stand. Nowhere, Kat. Never. Not once."

All at once she believed him. The blood ran out of her head. She felt it go. She felt it pool in her feet, where it throbbed in heavy, uncomfortable pulsations. She tried to speak, but no words came at first. After a moment she whispered an agonized, "Then where were you?"

That shuttered look she feared and hated came over his face. Though his gaze still met hers, she sensed he'd closed an important part of himself away somewhere . . . somewhere that she couldn't see it, and that he'd done it on purpose. "I had something . . . some thinking to do."

She pulled in a deep breath that felt as if it wanted to release itself in a scream. "But why?" she asked, her tone taut with pain.

"Why didn't I deny it? When you accused me?"

She nodded jerkily.

He made small, careful circles on the table with the handle of his spoon, looking at that, not at her. "I'm not entirely sure," he said. "Because your accusation hurt me pretty bad, for one thing. And because . . ."

"Because?" she prompted. He shrugged, and she had to fill in the blank. "Because you were looking for a way out? Of our marriage?"

He glanced at her, and the misery she felt was

reflected back to her from his eyes, from his soul. "It wasn't much of a marriage by then, Kat."

Her throat hurt so badly, she could hardly speak, but she forced herself. "I know it wasn't. But maybe it would have been a better marriage if you'd cared enough to deny my accusations. And tell me where you'd been."

He squeezed her hand. "And maybe if it had been a better marriage, you'd never have made that accusation."

She nodded. "But I believed what I said. When I said it. It was the only explanation I could come up with for your not being where you said you were supposed to be. I mean, it was the only explanation that made any sense."

"You seem . . . you seem to be ready to believe in me a little better now."

"Yes. It's funny, but I really do believe you now. Then, though, even if you'd denied everything, I probably wouldn't have accepted it, because . . ." She hesitated, looked down, then made herself face him again. "Because I didn't want to admit my own responsibility for our problems. I wasn't making home a very happy place for you. I hadn't for a long time. It was no wonder you wanted a . . . vacation away from me."

He touched her face with one fingertip, tracking a line from her eye to her chin. "None of it was all your fault, no more than it was all mine. Ah, Kat, don't cry, honey."

She blinked, surprised to find that she was, indeed, crying. "Please," he said, his voice cracking, "I really don't deal well with your tears."

She wiped her face on a crumpled paper napkin and

got awkwardly to her feet. "I'm really not dealing well with any of this, Rand. I'd like to go for a walk. Will you put the kids to bed, please?"

He sat looking up at her, then said, "Sure."

Without speaking again, Kat slipped out of his apartment.

When she got back, the house was dark but for one light in the living room. Rand looked up from the book he was reading, then stood. He walked over to her and held out his hand. She took it.

She could hear music playing softly on the stereo.

"Dance with me, Katherine," he said.

She moved into his arms, and he laid his cheek against hers. He was freshly shaven, smelled tangy and sexy and male. His body was hard, his need clearly outlined against her belly.

She rubbed her face on his smooth cheek, stroked her hands over his arms, molding the bulging muscles of his biceps. He cradled her, slipping his hands within the waistband of her jeans, touching the bare skin of her lower back. She sighed.

He sighed. The music soared, and they stood there with their feet unmoving, clinging to each other as they swayed in place, dancing a new kind of dance to an old kind of song.

Kat spoke at last, not looking at him. "Why didn't you tell me the truth, Rand? I mean in the past few weeks. There were ample opportunities."

He was silent for a minute, then sighed again and said, "I didn't think you'd believe me."

"What made tonight different?"

"I'm not sure. You seemed suddenly more . . . receptive to me. As if you'd quit fighting your feelings for me."

She looked up. "I had. I have. I love you."

His large frame shook within the circle of her arms. "Katherine . . ." It sounded like a prayer of thanksgiving. He held her tenderly, stroking his hands over her, filtering them through her hair, placing soft, whispering kisses against her temples, her cheeks, her throat, then holding her close again, still swaying to the music that filled both their souls.

"Come to bed with me," she said, her voice shaky, her face buried against his chest. "I want to make love with you, Rand."

He tilted her face up and smiled into her eyes, then brushed his mouth over hers. Her breath caught in her throat. He picked her up and carried her to her bedroom, setting her on her feet just inside. Pushing her up against the door, he closed it with the weight of their bodies against it.

Kissing her deeply, he reached behind her and gave the lock a quick turn. The snicking sound sent shivers of anticipation through Kat's body. She opened her mouth to his probing tongue, met it, and matched its forays. Then slowly, reluctantly, wavering between more and deeper kisses and the rest of what they needed, they broke apart.

"I love you, Katherine," he said, raising her hand and kissing the finger that wore his rings.

She met his gaze. "I love you, Rand."

He undid the ribbon that held her hair back. Her hair slithered, cool and scented, over his hands as he cupped the back of her neck. From the speakers in the corners of the bedroom, music continued to pulsate as desire pulsated through him. He tried to slake it with kisses, with caresses, but it grew and grew until it became his entire existence.

Kat laid her head on his shoulder as he pulled her away from the door and swept her into another almost-stepless dance. As he turned her, bending her backward, she caught sight of the room, which his shoulder had blocked from her view.

The light on her bedside table cast a soft glow over the brass bed. The covers were folded back. On one pillow lay a blood-red rose from one of the bushes he'd planted. On the other a box of condoms.

A low, husky laugh burbled out of her. "I see," she said. "I didn't have to ask. You had this planned."

He looked very serious. "I had it planned, Katherine. But, yes, you had to ask."

She cradled his face in her hands. "And if I hadn't?"

His smile held a tinge of pain. "Then you'd have come in here alone, seen my foolish preparations, and laughed at me."

She swallowed the thickness in her throat. "I wouldn't have laughed, Rand. Not at you. Never at you."

He drew in a long, unsteady breath. His eyes glittered as he molded the shape of her waist and hips. "And you did ask."

"I did, didn't I?" Her breathing quickened along with her heartbeat. "What—what are you going to do about it?"

"Lots of things," he said, nibbling at the soft skin under her chin. "Lots and lots of things. Slow, torturing things, things that will make you beg me to stop." He slid his hands into her hair, and they kissed again, long and ardent and provocative. "And things that will make you beg me not to stop."

She shuddered. "I . . . can't wait."

He smiled. "Ah, but you're going to have to."

ELEVEN

"You think so?" Kat pulled his head down and started a little sweet torture of her own.

She smiled when he finally broke away, tugging his earlobe from her teasing teeth. Their slow, sensuous dance had carried them to the side of the bed. She glanced at it, at the rose and the condoms. "It's nice to see my practical husband is trying to be romantic too."

He didn't correct her about their marital status, just smiled and slowly unbuttoned her blouse. When he was done, he picked up the rose and ran it from her hairline to the tip of her chin, then down between her breasts and over her stomach. "I'm sorry for all the flowers I didn't give you."

She took the rose and drew in its scent, then placed a kiss on the tip of the bud and transferred it to his lips. "I'm sorry for all the times when you might have and my attitude put you off."

He slipped the blouse off her shoulders and down her arms as he kissed her neck.

She tugged his T-shirt free of his pants and up over his head.

"Eager?" he asked, grinning as he emerged from the cloth.

She touched one of his nipples with the tip of her tongue, then raked her nails lightly down his chest. Both his nipples sprang taut. "Oh, yes." She turned him around and kissed the three little freckles below his shoulder blade, just to remind him they were there, and that he wasn't completely perfect. "You make me eager."

"You make me crazy." He wriggled under the assault of her lips on his back. When she ran the tip of her tongue down his spine to his waist, he whipped around to face her, catching her shoulders in his hands. "I want us to take our time, Kat."

She dragged her nails down his back, and his spine arched, thrusting his groin against her. "Really?" she asked.

"I'll show you what happens to teasing witches," he said as his belly clenched tight. His jeans were almost unbearably constricting, but he didn't dare loosen them, or the dance would be over before it began. His fingers shook as he fumbled with the front closure of her bra. When her breasts came free into his hands, he cupped them and lifted them. Bending, he licked first one, then the other.

Kat gasped at the feel of his tongue, rough on her nipples, sending shafts of sensation along nerves that culminated in her womb. Her abdominal muscles contracted, and she shuddered from deep inside.

Digging her fingers into his arms, she tasted the tang of his skin as her teeth bit gently at his shoulder.

Her left foot climbed up the back of his right leg, and he captured her knee in his hand, holding her leg high as he pushed his thigh against her center in rhythmic pulses.

Swiftly, in retaliation, she pressed her breasts to his naked chest, rubbing back and forth. He moaned and let her knee go, returned his mouth to her breasts, then down across her stomach. He sank to his knees, his lips tracing a line down her front until he met the barrier of her jeans.

Clasping her hips in his hands, he buried his face at the juncture of her thighs, the heat of his breath through the fabric sending a storm of desire through her.

He undid her jeans, pulling the waistband apart to slide the zipper down. He worked the pants slowly over her hips and down her legs, lifting her feet carefully to remove them.

Kat trembled and trembled, clinging to his shoulders, his head, as he kissed his way down to one knee, then back up from the other. His kisses burned her through her silky panties. He slipped one finger inside the elastic at her leg, stroking, parting, exploring.

"Enough," she gasped. "Please, that's enough." She groaned. She was doing exactly what he'd said he'd make her do, begging him to stop. But he had to. He had to, or it would be too much, and she'd die.

"Not yet," he said, and removed her panties. As he lifted her feet, each in turn, he kissed her toes. By the time he was done, her body quivered and glowed all over. He sat back on his haunches and looked at her.

"No," he muttered. "I won't do it. Never."

She gaped at him through her haze of desire. "What?" Her voice was a croaking sound.

"I'll buy you all the silk and lace you want," he said, running his hands over her body. "But not to wear to bed. I want you like this, Kat. All soft skin. All the sweet, pale colors that are you."

"Oh . . ." It was the most wildly, extravagantly romantic thing he had ever said to her, and the strange part was, she didn't think he had the faintest idea he was being romantic.

Rand smiled up at her radiant face, then let his gaze skim down over her breasts, rising and falling in time to her erratic breathing. He curved his hands around her thighs. His thumbs parted the pale, soft hair at the juncture of her legs and, finding her moist and slick and ready, he stroked her.

Her fingers sank into his hair, and she bent her knees until they touched his shoulders. He leaned closer, his hands wrapping around her tense buttocks. He kissed her belly, then drew his tongue down, down, and flicked at the hard, slippery center of her. She cried out sharply, her legs shaking within the clasp of his arms.

"Don't stop, don't stop, don't stop," she murmured. "Oh, please, don't ever stop."

She whispered his name like a chant and let her head fall back. Her hair tumbled over his arm as he lifted her to lay her on the bed. He kissed her thighs apart, kissed their inner surfaces. He kissed her belly again and would have tormented her further, but she dug her fingers into his shoulders and pulled herself up to a sitting position.

"I can't wait," she said, her eyes wild and unfocused. She clutched at his waist, fingers in his belt loops, pulling him between her legs. Her hips thrust in a rhythmic dance over which she had no control. "Please, oh, please, hurry. I need you, I need you, Rand. . . ."

"Sweetheart, I need you too," he said raggedly, fighting to get free of his pants. He felt as if he had thick gloves on, as if his fingers were numb inside them. "Help me."

Kat cried in choking sobs as she slapped his hands out of the way, stripped his jeans off him, then his bikini briefs. She lay back, gazing up at him. He was naked. Magnificently aroused. Hot. Kneeling over her, between her legs.

He caressed her intimately, probing with one finger, then two, and she squeezed her eyes shut. Her hands found his erection, and she stroked him, caressed him. He arched, twisting as if in pain too deep to bear. Freeing himself from her clasp, he lowered his body to hers.

"Help me," he said again, his voice guttural, cords in his neck standing out with strain. He thrust blindly and missed. She shifted as he thrust again, sending him father off the mark. Frustration grew as she tried to guide him, but their bodies refused to cooperate, to end the torment. It was as if they had forgotten how they best fit together, as if instinct, once trustworthy, had deserted them in their frenzy to unite. Rand tried to hold her writhing body still so his plunging hips could take control of their erratic motions. She complained.

He backed off. They stared at each other, and to Rand's delight, Kat's eyes filled with laughter. Her chuckle blended with his, and he cuddled her close, loving her more in that moment than ever before. She shifted slightly as he moved, and suddenly, more by accident than by design, they found their way back together.

"Ah, baby . . ." He thrust into her, then stopped. Raising up on his shaking arms, he stared at the box of condoms, half-crushed under her shoulder.

Kat grew utterly still as Rand froze over her, in her, afraid to move for fear she'd break a spell. What was he staring at? Then she felt it. The hard corner of the box of "practicality" he'd left on her bed.

"I don't care," she said, clasping him tightly lest he try to move away. "Rand, please!" She arched up to him, taking him fully into her, holding him there. She moved suggestively, her legs high around him as she clasped him in a lover's embrace. "If we make a baby tonight, we'll love it as much as we do the other two. Don't stop, my darling. Love me, Rand. Love me now!"

"Oh, God," he murmured, as if in awe, as if in fear, but it was too late for fears. He felt the tremors begin in her body, deep and hard. Felt her arch again, quaking, saw her head tossing from side to side.

"Don't stop, Kat," he groaned as he accepted the bite of her teeth in his shoulder, the incredible rock and roll of her hips. He tried to adapt to her motion, but it was so frantic, so out of control, there was no matching it. Instead, he mastered it. Held her. Took her.

Kat! Kat! Kat! He didn't know if he said her name aloud each time he thrust into her, he knew only that she was his, and he was hers, and there was no turning back from this moment.

He thrust again, and she moaned, clinging with her legs. He retreated, but she clamped her legs tighter, allowing him no freedom to move. Then, suddenly, he wanted none as the inside of her body turned to liquid, shimmering around him, drawing from him all that he could give.

When Kat opened her eyes, Rand was on one elbow, leaning over her, whispering her name. He brushed her hair back from her cheek with a tenderness that choked her throat with happiness.

She smiled and touched his lower lip. It looked slightly puffy, as if she might have bitten it. There was a mark on his shoulder too. She knew she'd bitten him there.

"My wild Kat," he said, a certain pride in his tone. "You're still pretty ferocious."

"Only when aroused." She traced the shape of his eyebrows. "And since I hadn't been aroused for nearly two-and-a-half years, I guess I had a lot of steam built up inside."

He lay back on the pillow, folded his arms behind his head, and stared at the ceiling. "You don't have to say things like that, Kat. My ego can handle your having had other men. Like I said before, we're divorced. I've had no claim on you."

She rose up on her elbow and looked at him. He didn't turn to meet her gaze. She pulled his face around until he did. His eyes were dark, bleak, and she could see that his ego wasn't half the man he thought it was.

"Why did you buy those condoms?" she asked.

He scowled. "Because you said you were off the pill. Dammit, Kat, I know you only married me because you were carrying Nathan. If we have any chance of getting back together permanently, this time I want it to be because you love me, not because I've knocked you up and you don't want an illegitimate kid on your hands."

Anger flashed through her. "That's a crummy thing to say!" She sat erect, folding her legs and pulling the sheet over her lap. With effort she curbed her temper. "I *did* marry you because I loved you!" She brushed her tangled hair off her brow. "Of all the dumb notions! It's usually the woman who thinks the man feels trapped by a premarital pregnancy. Why do you think I went off the pill?"

"I guess I never gave it any thought."

"I went off it because there was no need to stay on it. I wasn't at risk of pregnancy. I wasn't having sex with anyone. I didn't intend to have sex with anyone. I didn't want to have sex with anyone."

She lay back down beside him, folded her arms under her head, and stared at the ceiling, intentionally mimicking his earlier nonchalant pose. "I didn't want it until you moved back into the house, that is. Since then . . ." Her voice came out all tremulous. "Since then I've wanted nothing but. But I only wanted—want—it with you."

He rolled to his side, shoved the sheet down to her feet. "You want it, you got it." He touched his lips to the tip of her nose, the tip of her chin, then the tip of each breast. "But this time, with a condom, please."

"Leave?" Rand stared at the pants Kat held out to him.

"I'm sorry." She waggled his jeans in front of his nose. "I think it would be best. Before the kids get up."

"But they're going to know, Kat. We can't hide it from them. There's no need to hide it from them." He pushed his pants out of the way and gave her a darkly suspicious look. "Unless you had nothing more in mind than a one-night stand."

Kat wrapped her robe more tightly around herself and chewed on the inside of her cheek. She loved Rand. He loved her. But once before, that hadn't been enough to see them through the rough times. And something was still bothering her. Something she couldn't quite place.

She sank onto her bentwood rocker and fixed her gaze on his face. "I want more—far more—than a one-night stand. I want everything we had before, Rand."

He sat on the foot of the bed, returning her somber stare. "I want that, too, honey. I want it all. Only this time, I want us to do it right."

She frowned. "Right?"

A flicker of a smile hovered on his lips. A light shone in his eyes as if he were seeing the picture his words painted. "A church, swelling music, a minister in splendid robes, me standing by the altar all nervous and sweaty, my tie strangling me, and you . . ." His smile grew.

"You, Katherine, in a long white gown with a veil, drifting toward me, your eyes on mine. I want to wait for you there, then hold out my hand to you when you reach me, and hold you close to my side while we tell each other all those things we vowed once before."

Kat felt her mouth quiver. She widened her eyes in the hopes that the tears stinging them would go away. Sucking in a ragged breath, she tried to smile. It wobbled. "You want that?" she asked, astounded. "You?"

Rand watched the emotions playing over Kat's face. He could have told her the truth and said, *No, my darling, you want that, so I want to give it to you*, but he didn't. He continued to meet that wide, silvery gaze of hers and nodded. "I want that."

"Oh, Rand . . ."

He swallowed hard. It would have been so easy, eight years ago, for him to have given her that. It would have taken so little effort. But it was an effort he hadn't made. It had been easier to pretend not to see the disappointment in her eyes when he'd said he wanted to marry her the quickest way possible. "No muss, no fuss," was the way he'd put it. And Kat, loving him, had gone along with it.

He dropped to his knees before her. "So? What do you say? Do we go for it?" As he heard himself say the words, he knew he did want it, all the romantic trappings, the whole works, and not just for Kat. He wanted it for himself. Maybe if they had a proper wedding this time, the marriage would last.

Kat blinked and felt two tears escape. Rand reached out and flicked them away.

She stroked one hand down his cheek and let it slide to his shoulder, then onto his chest. Under her palm she felt his heart beating hard and fast. "I wonder how many women have received a proposal of marriage from a naked man on his knees?"

He caught her hand and pressed it to his cheek, his gaze never leaving her face. An expression closely resembling fear filled his eyes. "Why don't I hear you saying yes, Katherine?"

She clenched her teeth and swallowed hard. She couldn't maintain eye contact with him. Why wasn't she saying yes? It amazed her, delighted her, to know that he wanted what she did. So of course she should say yes. She should slide off that chair, onto her own knees before him, wrap him in her arms, and accept.

But . . . something held her back. She wished she could explain her hesitation to him. Maybe then she'd understand it herself.

"Katherine?"

She tried, knowing even as she heard them, how inadequate her words were. "I said I wanted it all, Rand, everything we had before. And I do. But I want, I think I want . . . something more as well." Because, if what they'd had before had been enough, why had things gone so wrong between them?

He got to his feet, confusion obvious on his face. "What more? What more is there?"

"I'm not sure," she said, pleating the sash of her robe between nervous fingers. "I'm not certain I can put it into words."

"Try."

She hesitated, searching for phrases she knew could never possibly convey what she felt on some deep, instinctive level. Where had these unwanted feelings come from? She wanted to be as clearheaded, as sure about what was right for herself as Rand was about what he wanted. But the conviction remained, unshakable, and she knew it would take more than a simple repetition of the words "I do" to eradicate it.

"I'm waiting," Rand said, and the hint of impatience in his tone told her he might not wait much longer.

"It's more like a . . . sense I have, a sense of—does this sound really crazy?—impending disaster if we don't take the time to think this through. It's an intuitive feeling that there's something missing."

She searched his eyes for any sign of understanding but saw none. Still, she felt some clarity enter her own emotional and mental disarray. Something missing. Yes, that was it. An absence of something. A lack.

Frustration harshened Rand's tone. "What could possibly be missing?"

Kat was unable to answer. She got to her feet and swung around to her dresser, picking up the silver-backed brush she'd inherited from her mother. She drew it through her hair, watching in the mirror, as Rand jammed one leg into his jeans, then the other, and dragged them up over his lean hips.

"From where I'm standing," he said, sliding up his zipper, "there wasn't a damn thing missing in the night we just spent together."

She whirled from the mirror. "That's not what I'm talking about!"

"No?" His glare held disbelief. His jaw went hard, the cleft in his chin deepening. "What else could you be talking about? We love each other, Kat. And we made love to each other. It was great for me. I thought it was for you, too, but maybe you've been taking acting lessons these past couple of years."

Ignoring her pained intake of breath, Rand rushed on, venting his hurt. "I gave you the best of me. If it wasn't good enough for you, if all you can do is bitch about it, maybe you better start looking elsewhere. And maybe I should too. After all, I've had the name for so long, why shouldn't I get to play the game?"

She slapped her brush onto the dresser. "That's not fair!"

"The hell it's not! What's not fair is your coming on to me like you did last night, then snatching it all back this morning. Well, lady, forget it! Just forget the whole damn thing! I'm outta here!"

He turned, grabbed his T-shirt and his briefs, and headed for the door.

"Rand."

He stopped, his hand on the knob. "What?"

She had to force herself to go on. "I'm not bitching, so don't walk away from me. That used to make me madder than almost anything, the way you walked out on an argument instead of seeing it through. I'm sorry if it sounded like I was complaining, but I wasn't. Our lovemaking lacked nothing. And I want more of it, lots, lots more."

Slowly, he turned back to her.

"But I don't want to rush into anything," she went on. "Until I'm sure that we can make it together again, in every way, it would be too unfair to the kids for us to give them any reason to hope. If we did let them know we were trying again, and we failed, what do you think it would do to them?"

Without waiting for a reply, she rushed on. "They'd never forgive us. You know that. We'd devastate them. I can't . . . I *won't* . . . put their happiness at risk."

Rand's dark gaze swept over her face. "What about mine, Kat? What about your own? After last night will you be happy to go back to sleeping alone?"

She knew she would not. "We can be together at night, Rand. But as for the rest, well, I need time. I need to reassess my feelings."

"Why? Mine are quite clear. I love you. I want to be with you all the time, openly, legitimately. I want us to be a family again, you, me, and our children."

"I want that too," she said. "But I have to wait. I'm not trying to be arbitrary here, or manipulative or anything. I'm not punishing you for something, if that's what you think. I don't like feeling this way. But whatever this sense of wrongness is that's eating at me, if I don't identify it and eliminate it before we become a couple again, I'm terrified it'll come up out of the dark some night and drive us apart."

"Then by all means," he said, his voice harsh and low with anger he tried to suppress, "take your time. Try to figure out what's going on in your warped female mind. I gave up on that one years ago."

He paused, breathing heavily. "But get this straight, Katherine. I will not sneak around, tiptoeing up here after the kids are in bed, sliding out again at dawn so they don't catch us sleeping together. And I won't have you coming to me, then leaving my bed in the middle of the night.

"When you're ready to talk sense, just let me know. In the meantime stay the hell out of my way. I can guarantee that my mood won't be one you'll like."

He turned back to the door and left.

"Hey," Rand said, knocking on Kat's office door the following evening. "Could I come in for a minute?"

Kat looked up from the papers she had spread around in an attempt to convince herself she was busy and productive. Rand wore his ragged cutoffs, a T-shirt with a hole near his navel, and no shoes. He brought the scent of the outdoors into the room with him. She forced her gaze from his powerful thighs and looked him square in the eye. "Depends," she said, "on your mood."

"Will you listen to an apology?"

She softened. "Sure. Come in."

"I've changed," he said, sinking onto the sofa and thrusting his long legs out, "but not so much that I've forgotten how to be a jerk when I can't have my own way. I said a few things yesterday morning that I'm not proud of. Such as your maybe taking acting lessons. I know your response to me was no fakery. And I know you're right. Unless we're very, very sure of what we're doing, we can't risk hurting the kids."

He sat erect and extended a hand to her. "Will you accept that I can still be a hardheaded S.O.B. at times and forgive me when I am? Please, Kat, can we at least be friends again?"

She accepted his hand. "I'll always be your friend, Rand, but I want to be your lover too."

His warm, firm clasp dropped away, as did his gaze. He stared at the floor for some moments, then looked up. "You know how much I want that, too, Katherine. I know you do." A muscle in his jaw jumped as he clenched his teeth. "But, probably with the same degree of instinctive conviction that tells you we have to be careful of how much we let the kids know, I know that I'm right too.

"I can't be your lover. There's a wrongness in that for me. I'm . . . afraid, Kat."

She sat regarding the top of his bowed head for a long, silent time, remembering how she'd laughed and told Todd that Rand was afraid of nothing. She'd believed it when she said it. She'd always seen Rand as invincible. Always believed he saw himself in that light. It touched her for him to open himself that much, to risk saying such a thing to her.

"What are you afraid of?"

He looked up. "That if we don't have it all, the wedding, the rings, the certificate all done up in fancy calligraphy that says what we have together is real—it won't *be* real. That if we aren't married and things start to go wrong for us again, even in the slightest way, you'll simply walk away."

"Rand . . ." She rose and went to sit beside him. Her bare thigh brushed against his. He moved away from her, leaving her feeling bereft. She went on regardless of her hurt. "We were married, remember? We had the rings, the piece of paper. And we walked away from each other despite all that. They didn't protect our marriage when we stopped trying to tough things out together. What makes you so sure they would another time?"

He shrugged. "I didn't say it was a rational feeling. Just a very real one. I believe right down in my gut that if we remarry, it will be forever this time. I believe just as strongly that if we don't, if we let ourselves drift into a relationship without giving it strong parameters, safe barriers to outside influences, we could too easily drift out of it again."

"Outside influences?"

He nodded. "Not other men. Nor other women. I think we've moved beyond worrying about things like that. But . . . there's the past. It's always with m—us. It could reach out and drive wedges between us as easily as those nebulous doubts of yours."

The past? She wondered. He'd almost said, "it's always with me," then he'd changed it. What about the past—his past—worried him? How could it affect their present-day lives, or their future?

After a time she nodded. "I guess I have to live with it, don't I? It's your decision, and you have as much right to make it as I had to make the one I did."

"But friends?" he asked again. "That's still okay?"

She smiled. "That's still okay."

He stood and walked to the door. "Good. Because I have something for my friend." He reached out into the hallway and brought in a brightly wrapped box with a big blue bow on top.

"For you, Kat."

She held it on her lap as she looked at him quizzically. "It's not my birthday."

"I know that. Just open it, will you?" He scowled, as impatient as Nathan would have been, his eyes as eager.

She did as he asked, lifted the lid, and folded back layers of tissue paper. "Oh, my . . ." she whispered, lifting out the silk garment. It was long, and soft, and filmy, a delicate shade of green at the shoulders, deepening toward the hem.

"It's not the same as the one you wanted before," Rand said as she dropped the box and stood to hold the caftan up to herself. "But I hope it'll do."

She gazed at him through a shimmer of tears. "Dammit," she whispered. "What are you trying to do, Waddle? Seduce me all over again?"

He shook his head and slid his arms around her, holding her gently, no seduction, no sexuality at all in his embrace. "Uh-uh," he murmured against her hair. "I'm trying to fill in for you whatever pieces you find missing."

Then he crushed her tightly to him, rocking her back and forth. "I want us to be whole again, babe! I want it so badly, I think I'll die if we don't find our way back to each other."

Kat could only cling to him and want the same.

TWELVE

Kat discovered during the next two weeks that receiving romantic gifts because she'd told Rand that she liked them made them no less romantic. Maybe, she decided the day he gave her an enormous box of chocolates, it was even more romantic, because it meant he was willing to go out of his way to please her. It meant he was thinking about her.

As she thought about him constantly. She ached with wanting him, needing him, knowing he was only down one flight of stairs and that if she really set her mind to it, she could end up in his bed within the space of five minutes. But, as he had refused to seduce her to get his own way, she refused to do the same.

Where, she wondered, was it all going to end?

That he suffered to the same degree as she did, she knew. That he found it as difficult as she did not to give in to the forces constantly drawing them together was no secret. He'd taken to going out in the evenings.

She didn't ask where, but she knew on a gut level that he was only visiting friends.

She watched his car leave one evening shortly after he'd tucked the kids in, then went into the backyard where she worked for an hour until the light faded completely. Inside, she showered, changed into her green caftan, and drifted around the too-confining house.

Restless, she poured herself a glass of wine and sat on the patio to watch the stars come out, her longing for Rand growing ever more intense. Needing action, she went back inside, put a CD in the player, and danced by herself, absorbing the sensuous beat into her every fiber until it filled her totally.

She flung out her arms and spun in a dizzying circle, the filmy silk of her caftan caressing her bare legs. She snapped her fingers and threw back her head, swaying to the erotic tempo.

Then, with a shiver of pure excitement, she closed her eyes and wrapped her arms around herself.

That's what Rand would do. She rubbed her hands up over her bare shoulders inside the wide sleeves. He'd do that, too, and more. Her breasts ached, and her nipples puckered into hard, painful nubs. Oh, how she wanted to dance with Rand! She wanted the closeness, she wanted his touch, and she wanted what the dancing would lead to. She spun around dizzily, the music hammering in her blood, in her heart.

Dance music. It could drive a man insane. Rand ground his molars together as he sat at his computer and listened to the hot beat of a Latin guitar drifting down from the floor above. Was she doing it on purpose to cause him this agony? He shut the door to block out the sound of the suggestive rhythm, but it didn't help. The pounding music went on, and he couldn't stand it.

He stomped to the bathroom, flinging off his clothes on the way, and stepped into the shower. He let the water drown out the sound, but the beat hammered on in his blood. He ached. He yearned. Groaning, he twisted the hot water off and cranked the cold tap on full, letting icy spray sluice over his body.

Ten minutes later he stood toweling his hair, and the music continued as before. Cursing he wrapped the towel around his hips and strode out of the suite. She had no conscience! It was time to put a stop to it.

He didn't bother knocking, and Kat happened to be facing the door when Rand flung it open.

She took a faltering step back, her gaze on his thunderous face. He strode into the room, fists clenched at his sides, a muscle pulsing in his jaw. Stopping in front of her, he closed his eyes tightly, swayed for a moment, and opened them again.

He reached for her, catching her in his arms, bending his head, and clamping his mouth to hers.

Elation soared along with desire as Kat clung to him. His towel was no impediment to the rising tide of his need. The hard evidence of his passion inflamed her, and she pulled him close to her, breathing deeply of his fresh-from-the-shower scent. He smelled wonderful. His skin was damp; his hair, as she tunneled her fingers through it, still wet. His mouth was hungry on hers, and he fed from her for a long time.

At last he broke their kiss but filled his hands with her hair and held her head so she couldn't move away.

"I came to give you hell," he said, breathing hard, his voice rough. "I came to tell you to shut off the music. I came to say it was too loud." He realized as he said it that it wasn't too loud. Conversation was quite comfortable, the music providing a nice background for it.

Kat's chest rose and fell at the same quick rate as his. Her blood pounded through her veins, heating her skin, echoing in her head, giving her a frothy, dizzy sensation. "Oh, yes?" she said encouragingly.

"Oh, yes." His eyes glittered. "But now . . . I guess maybe I want to dance."

"Really?"

"Really." He lifted her, the silk of her caftan gliding up over her thighs, draping across his arm and hand like a whispered promise. He carried her to her room, set her in the middle of the bed, and lay with her.

They "danced" until a pale light came through the curtains and a chorus of birds sang them to sleep.

"This is the way it's going to be, isn't it?" Rand asked, retrieving his crumpled towel from the bedroom floor a couple of hours later. "I'll come here at night and leave in the morning."

Kat searched his face, reading the depth of his unhappiness. "Not if you don't want to come here, Rand."

He tucked the towel around his hips. "But I do want to. That's the trouble. I can't stop wanting."

She wished she could agree to give him everything he wanted. She went to him, held him, loving him with frightening intensity. It would be so easy to say, Yes, I'll marry you again.

It would be so easy . . . and so wrong. "I feel I'm being terribly unfair to you."

"Don't worry about it, sweetheart," he said, and she felt strange that he was comforting her. It should be the other way around. "We'll work it out." He tipped her face up and smiled at her. "One of my sainted mother's favorite sayings was, 'Kid, life's not always fair.' "

Kat went still, stunned to hear him speak so lightly of his mother. It shocked her to hear him speak of her at all. It also emboldened her to ask a question she'd long wanted answered. "What—what do you suppose your mother would think of me?"

That dreaded shuttered look slipped over his eyes, and for a moment she was sure he wouldn't answer, would change the subject. But though the shadows remained in his eyes, he said slowly, as if he were thinking his words out before he uttered them, "I think she'd have liked you. You don't take any guff from anyone."

Kat gnawed on her lower lip. "Did she?" she asked tentatively, almost holding her breath.

This time, the shutter came down fully. Rand let her go and half turned away, readjusting his towel. "I'll make breakfast for the kids," he said. "You try to catch a bit more sleep before work."

"No!" she said quickly, jerking her robe on, disappointment stinging. Why had she asked that particular question? A different one might have kept the conversation going. "You go back down. I'll take care of the kids."

He frowned at her. "Kat? What's the matter? Why are you mad?"

Dammit, dammit, dammit! He genuinely did not know! Honesty, something she valued highly, fled under his bewildered stare. What good would it do to accuse him of shutting her out? He'd only deny it.

"I need some time with the kids, too, you know. And lately I hardly see them. They'd rather be with you, even when I'm at home." She scowled at him. "They certainly prefer your cooking." Especially since he'd started barbecuing.

He sat down on the edge of the bed. "Does that bother you, Kat? Their liking my cooking?"

She slumped into the rocker across from him. "Sometimes. In a way."

"In what way?"

She threw her hands up and shot to her feet. Shooing him off the bed, she straightened the sheets and dragged the duvet up. "I don't . . ." She saw him on the far side of the bed, plumping a pillow. His expression told her that a weak *I don't know* wasn't something he was prepared to accept from her.

"All right," she said, smashing her fist into the pillow she held. "Sometimes I feel . . . redundant. I mean, you keep the house spotless. You've taken over the laundry, the yard work, most of the child care.

"They're my kids, too, Rand, and I'm beginning to feel like an interloper in my own home."

It was his turn to fling his hands up as he made a disgusted, frustrated sound. "For the love of Harry, Katherine! You always maintained you wanted help with the housework, wanted me to take a greater interest in the kids! Now that you've got it, you're complaining?"

"No." She firmed her chin. "What I'm trying to say is that I never wanted someone to take over for me. I wanted you to *share* things with me, just as I was sharing the income-earning with you.

"You said I'd rob you of your manhood if I didn't let you pay support for the kids. You're robbing me of something, too, though I'm not sure what to call it, by doing everything around the house, and doing it better than I do. I used to think you wanted me to turn into your mother. Now, I feel as if you've turned into her instead, as if you're trying to show me up by being a better mother than I ever was. Maybe even a better mother than she was. If that were possible."

His shoulders slumped. His hands clenched at his sides. He stared at her for perhaps a full sixty seconds as the color ebbed and flowed in his face, finally leaving it white to the lips.

"My mother," he said clearly, softly, "was a hooker."

With his head high he opened the door, stepped through it, and closed it behind him. Kat stared at its panels, wondering if she had just experienced an incredibly erotic and graphic nightlong dream with a twisted, bitter surprise ending. She stumbled from bed to rocking chair before her knees collapsed.

"Mom?" Nathan opened her door. "Who were you talking to?"

"I'm not entirely certain," she said. "Not certain at all."

"Mom?" He slid his warm hand into hers. "Know what? You're kinda weird sometimes. Can you make breakfast now?"

"Can we discuss it?"

Kat presented herself at Rand's door the minute she returned from walking the kids to school.

He stepped back to let her in. The door to his workroom was open, and she saw the blue screen of his computer activated for his daily work.

"If you have time, that is."

He looked wary. "Don't you have to go to work?"

She shrugged. "If a vice president can't take a day off for a family emergency, then who can?"

He shut the door. "You can't exactly call it an emergency, Kat. My mother was a prostitute for a long time, and it was a long time ago. I survived it then. I discovered this morning that I can survive your knowing it."

His mouth twisted up on one side, and he made a short sound that might have been a laugh. "More or less."

Kat sat down on the chintz ottoman and pressed her hands between her knees. "Why did you lie to me about her? Why did you spend all that energy making up stories about how wonderful she was, what a perfect home you came from?"

He sat on the couch. "I didn't lie, Kat. I just let you believe what you wanted to believe."

"No." Her eyes accused him. "In order to move back in here with us, you tried to justify not telling the truth about your finances by saying you only let me go on believing what I already did. It won't wash this time, Rand.

"You let me believe what *you wanted* me to believe. You went out of your way to make sure I thought you had an exemplary mother, a *Father Knows Best* upbringing. Dammit, Rand, I need to know why."

She'd thought long and deeply on her way back home from taking the children to school. She knew now what the missing element was. Trust. Rand's trust—or lack of it—for her. In her. If he couldn't confide in her, they would never achieve the closeness she knew was necessary for their marriage to work for her.

She'd considered not asking, waiting to see what else he would divulge on his own. She'd told him she wanted romantic gestures and had gotten them. But weren't confidences different? He couldn't pretend when it came to tangible objects like flowers and candy and beautiful clothes. He could, though, continue to make up stories he thought might appease her curiosity.

This was too big, too important. She simply had to know.

"Why?" she asked again, quietly but insistently. "Why the lies?"

She thought he wouldn't answer. He got up, walked to the kitchen, and poured himself some coffee. As an afterthought, he poured some for her too. He slid it across the counter toward her when she followed him.

"Shame," he said, sitting on the chair behind the table. "I grew up with shame.

"You'll never know what it was like. I was raised in a whorehouse. Oh, they didn't call it that, my mother and her 'waitresses,' any more than they called themselves prostitutes. They called it the Tricorn Inn. It was on the outskirts of Whitehorse, and as long as they kept the action clean, the authorities turned a blind eye. But everyone knew. I knew from the time I was about Nathan's age what went on upstairs."

She leaned on the counter, watching him, her hands wrapped around her coffee mug. She felt as icy cold as if she were in Whitehorse.

"I loved school because I could escape," he went on. "Books." He smiled wryly. "They were my best friends, the only friends I would admit into my life. I used to walk three miles into town to the library on weekends because I could hide there. No one in the books I read knew what went on in my home. The characters I identified with never had to live with shame. When I was with fictional characters, I became a fictional character. I could hold my head up.

"When I was sixteen, I left the Yukon. I put it behind me and swore I'd never go back. I made up a story about my home that was like the ones I'd read as a little kid, where there was a mother who wore an apron and baked bread and a dad who wore a suit and tie and went to work in the morning and came home at night and gave his paycheck to his wife. I used to think someday I'd get a dog and call him Mr. Muggs, and my children would roll around on the floor with him, laughing."

Kat bit her lip and lowered herself into a chair across from him. "And I never wanted a dog."

He shrugged. "No matter. The dog was as much a fantasy as the perfect little aproned wife I'd dreamed up for myself. As much a pretense as the childhood home I'd created in my mind, one that I could be proud of. Parents who didn't make me hide my head. Parents who wouldn't turn off the nice girls I wanted to date. A home I could bring my friends to.

"I made up a fantasy and used it to answer the inevitable questions people ask when they first meet someone. By the time I met you, I guess I'd almost come to believe it myself. I fed it to you, and you swallowed it whole. And why wouldn't you? You were such a nice girl, you couldn't contemplate a person coming from the kind of home I had."

He saw the denial spark in her eyes and put his fingers over her mouth. "Oh, I know your parents got divorced. I know your father left your mother for a younger woman, but to me, that seemed so tame as to be normal. It was almost like a fantasy to me too. I don't think I realized until I saw how much our divorce hurt our kids that you had been seriously traumatized by your dad leaving your mother and abandoning you at the same time.

"That's why I quit the foreign desk, so I could be as close to Nathan and Katie as possible."

Kat got up and returned to the living room, curling in the corner of the couch. Rand remained at the table until he'd finished his coffee.

"What are you thinking?" he asked as he came to sit beside her.

"I'm not sure. Lots of things. Your father. You said 'parents' you didn't have to be ashamed of. Did you know him?"

He snorted, a harsh, bitter sound. "Know him? Of course I did. He was the proprietor. I'm not sure if he and my mother were married legally, but she used his name."

The gaze he turned on her made her ache for him. "So did I. Do I. And you. And our children. I should have changed it to something else. How do you like bearing the name of a man who did nothing but sit in the lounge all day drinking? And pimping.

"He bragged about what an easy life he had, living off what my mother earned on her back. The customers paid *him* before they went upstairs, and he was big enough, beefy enough, to make sure they did. He was also big enough and beefy enough to have stopped the entire business if he'd chosen to.

"I used to want to kill him for not stopping it, for not protecting my mother from those men and their depravity. It took me until I was sixteen to admit to myself that things were the way they were because *she* wanted them to be. My parents, both of them, were as depraved as any of their customers."

"So, I decided that I would be the best, most protective husband in the world if only I could find a woman who would be the best kind of wife and mother. But what I didn't know was that I wanted a wife who would mother me as well as my children."

She was silent for a few minutes. "I never once guessed that you wanted me to mother you." Pity for him warred with the remnants of her old resentment as the latter sparked and took flame. "Who the hell could mother an egotistical, bossy man who wanted to make all the decisions, make all the rules?"

Rand drew in a deep breath and let it go. "I don't know. I know I asked too much of you."

"Too much? Or not enough? Why didn't you tell me you needed compassion from me—understanding, nurturing? Don't you think if you'd come clean about your childhood, I might have understood you better, been more likely to give you what you wanted? Why did you think it was enough to tell me that your parents died when you were sixteen? Didn't you think I deserved to know the whole truth?"

He shoved himself up and paced the small living area. "They didn't die when I was sixteen. I lied about that too."

"My God!" She shot to her feet. "What else have you lied about, Rand? Was our whole life together based on a fantasy?"

He shrugged. "I guess you could put it that way. The old man died of cirrhosis a year or so after I left. *She* died a few months before you left me. Somebody— a lawyer—tracked me down through the newspaper. She'd left me the inn."

He turned from her and stared out the window at the irises they had planted together in the backyard. Kat looked beyond him, watching the tall purple heads wave in the breeze against the neatly clipped grass, above a perfectly aligned gray stone wall. It was a clean, orderly scene, with neat edges, secure borders, quite unlike the roiling disorder in her mind.

"I had to go back, Kat," he said, facing her again. "I had to go and . . . dispose of the inn." His eyes were so dark, they appeared black in his pale face. "And I still didn't want you to know. So I couldn't tell you."

She closed her eyes as full understanding flooded her on a wave of incomparable pain. "So you took emergency personal leave from the paper and went to the Yukon." She slumped to the sofa.

"Yes."

She opened her eyes. "Even when I accused you of having been with another woman, you couldn't tell me the truth?"

"I was just so ashamed."

"So ashamed, you let our marriage blow apart. That wasn't shame, Rand. That was pride."

He shrugged again. "I don't know, Katherine. Maybe it was. I knew only I couldn't tell you the truth."

He gazed broodingly at her. "And our marriage had already blown apart. It blew apart for me the moment you accused me of infidelity. I figured you loved me despite our differences. And I thought you trusted me. It hurt worse than I've ever been hurt to know you believed I could do that to you. Especially when, as things got worse and worse between us, and I was tempted to go to another woman for . . . comfort, I never did. I felt betrayed when you accused me. It had always been really important that you trusted me because I tried so hard to be a good man, different from my father."

"Trust?" She stared at him as she leaped to her feet. "How can you talk to me of trust when you didn't trust me enough to tell me the truth about your background?"

He shook his head in despair. "I knew most marriages went through bad patches. I believed we'd make it through ours, come out the other side, and when you were willing to talk to me again, willing to listen, willing to trust, I could fix it all without resorting to telling you the truth about me. I didn't want to hurt you. I wanted to protect you from the dirt that had soiled my life. I wanted to protect our kids. As for the other, I thought that, in time, you'd forgive me for what you believed I'd done."

She laughed bitterly as she crossed the room to the door, then paused by the tacky coat tree. "You know, I remember my father saying exactly the same thing to my mother and me the day he told us he was leaving. He said he'd never wanted to hurt us, so he had lied."

She stared at Rand. "But he, just like you, lied not to protect the people he professed to care about, but to protect himself."

She rocked the coat tree. "At least this makes sense now. It was a relic from your past." She turned to face him again. "Like the lies, Rand, it's ugly and dirty and cheap."

He nodded. "I know."

Silently, they looked at each other, Rand by the window, Kat by the door, on the verge of leaving. Something held her there. She couldn't have said what.

Rand smiled crookedly. "I'm waiting for you to leave, you know. I'm almost holding my breath, waiting. In a way I think I want you to go. Because then I'll be able to run. Be able to hide. Be able to pretend that this conversation never took place, pretend you don't know the ugly truth about me. Because you see, if you leave, I won't have to say, can you forgive me for all the lies? Can we start over again, this time with the truth between us?"

Kat continued to stand there, looking at him. She took one tentative step toward him, stopped, then took another. When she reached him, she stood before him, not touching. "No. No, we can't start over again with the truth between us. I don't want anything between us. The truth can surround us, Rand. It can bind us together."

He inhaled harshly and put his hands on her shoulders, almost, she thought, afraid to believe.

"When my dad told us," she went on, "that his mistress was pregnant and he was moving in with her, I lived with what I thought was the worst kind of shame a person could suffer. I hadn't wanted to think of my father as having sex with anyone, let alone a woman only five or six years my senior. I think I have a small, partial idea of how much greater your feelings of shame must have been."

He dropped his hands to her waist, and suddenly they were clinging together, both shaking as if with chills, holding each other protectively, hoping the power of their love could ward off future evil.

"What did you do with the inn?" Kat asked when their trembling had abated. She reached up and wiped away the tears streaking Rand's face. She had never seen him cry before.

"Sold it," he said. "There was nothing I wanted from it." He smiled wryly and glanced across the room. "Well, one thing."

Together, they looked at the coatrack. The finger still jutted up in its unmistakable gesture of defiance.

Kat cradled his cheek with one hand. "Let's take it upstairs. We'll put it in the front hall. When our guests ask about it, we'll smile at each other and be very, very mysterious, and we'll never tell a soul."

" 'We'?" he said. " 'Our' guests? I like your pronouns, Ms. Waddell."

"Uh, could we make that *Mrs.* Waddell, please?"

"Oh, baby . . ." He kissed her, then lifted his head and smiled at her. "I love your choice of honorific, *Mrs.* Waddell."

She pouted. "Don't you love anything besides that?"

"Well, I don't know," he said. "What else have you got?"

Kat showed him.

He loved it.

THE EDITOR'S CORNER

Along with the May flowers come six fabulous Loveswepts that will dazzle you with humor, excitement, and, above all, love. Touching, tender, packed with emotion and wonderfully happy endings, our six upcoming romances are real treasures.

The ever-popular Charlotte Hughes leads things off with **THE DEVIL AND MISS GOODY TWO-SHOES**, LOVESWEPT #684. Kane Stoddard had never answered the dozens of letters Melanie Abercrombie had written him in prison, but her words had kept his spirit alive during the three years he'd been jailed in error—and now he wants nothing more than a new start, and a chance to meet the woman who touched his angry soul. Stunned by the sizzling attraction she feels for Kane, Mel struggles to deny the passionate emotions Kane's touch awakens. No one had ever believed in Kane until Mel's sweet caring makes him dare to taste her innocent lips, makes him hunger to hold her until the sun rises. He can only hope that his fierce loving will vanquish her fear of losing him. Touching and intense, **THE DEVIL AND MISS GOODY TWO-SHOES** is the kind of love story that Charlotte is known and loved for.

This month Terry Lawrence delivers some **CLOSE ENCOUNTERS**, LOVESWEPT #685—but of the romantic kind. Alone in the elevator with his soon-to-be ex-wife, Tony Paretti decides he isn't giving Sara Cohen up without a fight! But when fate sends the elevator plunging ten floors and tosses her into his arms, he seizes his chance—and with breath-stealing abandon embraces the woman he's never stopped loving. Kissing Sara with a savage passion that transcends pain, Tony insists that what they had was too good to let go, that together they are strong enough to face the grief that shattered their marriage. Sara aches to rebuild the bonds of their love but doesn't know if she can trust him with her sorrow, even after Tony confesses the secret hopes that he's never dared to tell another soul. Terry will have you crying and cheering as these two people discover the courage to love again.

Get ready for a case of mistaken identity in **THE ONE FOR ME**, LOVESWEPT #686, by Mary Kay McComas. It was a ridiculous masquerade, pretending to be his twin brother at a business dinner, but Peter Wesley grows utterly confused when his guest returns from the powder room—and promptly steals his heart! She looks astonishingly like the woman he'd dined with earlier, but he's convinced that the cool fire and passionate longing in her bright blue eyes is new and dangerously irresistible. Katherine Asher hates impersonating her look-alike sisters, and seeing Peter makes her regret she'd ever agreed. When he kisses her with primitive yearning, she aches to admit her secret—that she wants him for herself! Once the charade is revealed, Peter woos her with fierce pleasure until she surrenders. She has always taken her happiness last, but is she ready to put her love for him first? **THE ONE FOR ME** is humorous and hot—just too good to resist.

Marcia Evanick gives us a hero who is **PLAYING FOR KEEPS**, LOVESWEPT #687. For the past two years detective Reece Carpenter has solved the fake murder-mystery at the Montgomery clan's annual family reunion, infuriating the beautiful—and competitive—Tennessee Montgomery. But when he faces his tempting rival this time, all he wants to win is her heart! Tennie has come prepared to beat her nemesis if it kills her—but the wild flames in his eyes light a fire in her blood that only his lips can satisfy. Tricked into working as a team, Tennie and Reece struggle to prove which is the better sleuth, but the enforced closeness creates a bigger challenge: to keep their minds on the case when they can't keep their hands off each other! Another keeper from Marcia Evanick.

STRANGE BEDFELLOWS, LOVESWEPT #688, is the newest wonderful romance from Patt Bucheister. John Lomax gave up rescuing ladies in distress when he traded his cop's mean streets for the peace of rural Kentucky, but he feels his resolve weaken when he discovers Silver Knight asleep on his couch! Her sea nymph's eyes brimming with delicious humor, her temptress's smile teasingly seductive, Silver pleads with him to probe a mystery in her New York apartment—and her hunk of a hero is hooked! Fascinated by her reluctant knight, an enigmatic warrior whose pain only she can soothe, Silver wonders if a joyous romp might help her free his spirit from the demons of a shadowy past. He is her reckless gamble, the dare she can't refuse—but she needs to make him understand his true home is in her arms. **STRANGE BEDFELLOWS** is Patt Bucheister at her sizzling best.

And last, but certainly not least, is **NO PROMISES MADE**, LOVESWEPT #689, by Maris Soule. Eric Newman is a sleek black panther of a man who holds Ashley Kehler spellbound, mesmerizing her with a look that strips her bare and caresses her senses, but he could also make her lose control, forget the dreams that drive her . . . and Ashley knows she must resist this seducer who ignites a fever in her blood! Drawn to this golden spitfire who is his opposite in every way, Eric feels exhilarated, intrigued against his will—but devastated by the knowledge that she'll soon be leaving. Ashley wavers between ecstasy and guilt, yet Eric knows the only way to keep his love is to let her go, hoping that she is ready to choose the life that will bring her joy. Don't miss this fabulous story!

Happy reading!

With warmest wishes,

Nita Taublib

Nita Taublib

Associate Publisher

P.S. Don't miss the exciting women's novels from Bantam that are coming your way in May—**DECEPTION**, by Amanda Quick, is the paperback edition of her first *New York Times* bestselling hardcover; **RELENTLESS**, by award-winning author Patricia Potter, is a searing tale of revenge and desire, set in Colorado during the 1870's; **SEIZED BY LOVE**, by Susan Johnson, is a novel of savage passions and dangerous pleasures sweeping from fabulous country estates and hunting lodges to the opulent ballrooms and salons of Russian nobility; and **WILD CHILD**, by bestselling author Suzanne Forster, reunites adversaries who share a tangled past—and for whom an old spark of conflict will kindle into a dangerously passionate blaze. We'll be giving you a sneak peek at these terrific books in next month's LOVESWEPTs. And immediately following this page look for a preview of the exciting romances from Bantam that are *available now*!

Don't miss these exciting books by your favorite Bantam authors

On sale in March:

DARK PARADISE
by *Tami Hoag*

WARRIOR BRIDE
by *Tamara Leigh*

REBEL IN SILK
by *Sandra Chastain*

"Ms. Hoag has deservedly become one of the romance genre's most treasured authors."
—*Rave Reviews*

Look For

DARK PARADISE

by

Tami Hoag

Here is nationally bestselling author Tami Hoag's most dangerously erotic novel yet, a story filled with heart-stopping suspense and shocking passion . . . a story of a woman drawn to a man as hard and untamable as the land he loves, and to a town steeped in secrets—where a killer lurks.

Night had fallen by the time Mari finally found her way to Lucy's place with the aid of the map Lucy had sent in her first letter. Her "hide-out," she'd called it. The huge sky was as black as velvet, sewn with the sequins of more stars than she had ever imagined. The world suddenly seemed a vast, empty wilderness, and she pulled into the yard of the small ranch, questioning for the first time the wisdom of a surprise arrival. There were no lights glowing a welcome in the windows of the handsome new log house. The garage doors were closed.

She climbed out of her Honda and stretched, feeling exhausted and rumpled. The past two weeks had sapped her strength, the decisions she had made taking chunks of it at a time. The drive up from Sacramento had been accomplished in a twenty-four hour marathon with breaks for nothing more than the bathroom and truck stop burritos, and now the physical strain of that weighed her down like an anchor.

It had seemed essential that she get here as quickly as possible, as if she had been afraid her nerve would give out and she would succumb to the endless dissatisfaction of her life in California if she didn't escape immediately. The wild pendulum her emotions had been riding had left her feeling drained and dizzy. She had counted on falling into Lucy's care the instant she got out of her car, but Lucy didn't appear to be home, and disappointment sent the pendulum swinging downward again.

Foolish, really, she told herself, blinking back the threat of tears as she headed for the front porch. She couldn't have expected Lucy to know she was coming. She hadn't been able to bring herself to call ahead. A call would have meant an explanation of everything that had gone on in the past two weeks, and that was better made in person.

A calico cat watched her approach from the porch rail, but jumped down and ran away as she climbed the steps, its claws scratching the wood floor as it darted around the corner of the porch and disappeared. The wind swept down off the mountain and howled around the weathered outbuildings, bringing with it a sense of isolation and a vague feeling of desertion that Mari tried to shrug off as she raised a hand and knocked on the door.

No lights brightened the windows. No voice called out for her to keep her pants on.

She swallowed at the combination of disappointment and uneasiness that crowded at the back of her throat. Against her will, her eyes did a quick scan of the moon-shadowed ranch yard and the hills beyond. The place was in the middle of nowhere. She had driven through the small town of New Eden and gone miles into the wilderness, seeing no more than two other houses on the way—and those from a great distance.

She knocked again, but didn't wait for an answer before trying the door. Lucy had mentioned wildlife in her few letters. The four-legged, flea-scratching kind.

"Bears. I remember something about bears," she muttered, the nerves at the base of her neck wriggling at the possibility that there were a dozen watching her from the cover of darkness, sizing her up with their beady little eyes while their stomachs growled. "If it's all the same to you, Luce, I'd rather not meet one up close and personal while you're off doing the boot scootin' boogie with some cowboy."

Stepping inside, she fumbled along the wall for a light switch, then blinked against the glare of a dozen small bulbs artfully arranged in a chandelier of antlers. Her first thought was that Lucy's abysmal housekeeping talents had deteriorated to a shocking new low. The place was a disaster area, strewn with books, newspapers, note paper, clothing.

She drifted away from the door and into the great room that encompassed most of the first floor of the house, her brain stumbling to make sense of the contradictory information it was getting. The house was barely a year old, a blend of Western tradition and contemporary architectural touches. Lucy had hired a decorator to capture those intertwined feelings in the interior. But the western watercolor prints on the walls hung at drunken angles. The cushions had been torn from the heavy, overstuffed chairs. The seat of the red leather sofa had been slit from end to end. Stuffing rose up from the wound in ragged tufts. Broken lamps and shattered pottery littered the expensive Berber rug. An overgrown pothos had been ripped from its planter and shredded, and was strung across the carpet like strips of tattered green ribbon.

Not even Lucy was this big a slob.

Mari's pulse picked up the rhythm of fear. "Lucy?" she called, the tremor in her voice a vocal extension of the goosebumps that were pebbling her arms. The only answer was an ominous silence that pressed in on her eardrums until they were pounding.

She stepped over a gutted throw pillow, picked her way around a smashed terra cotta urn and peered into the darkened kitchen area. The refrigerator door was ajar, the light within glowing like the promise of gold inside a treasure chest. The smell, however, promised something less pleasant.

She wrinkled her nose and blinked against the sour fumes as she found the light switch on the wall and flicked it upward. Recessed lighting beamed down on a repulsive mess of spoiling food and spilled beer. Milk puddled on the Mexican tile in front of the refrigerator. The carton lay abandoned on its side. Flies hovered over the garbage like tiny vultures.

"Jesus, Lucy," she muttered, "what kind of party did you throw here?"

And where the hell are you?

The pine cupboard doors stood open, their contents spewed out of them. Stoneware and china and flatware lay broken and scattered. Appropriately macabre place settings for the gruesome meal that had been laid out on the floor.

Mari backed away slowly, her hand trembling as she reached out to steady herself with the one ladder-back chair that remained upright at the long pine harvest table. She caught her full lower lip between her teeth and stared through the sheen of tears. She had worked too many criminal cases not to see this for what it was. The house had been ransacked. The motive could have been robbery or the destruction could have been the aftermath of something else, something uglier.

"Lucy?" she called again, her heart sinking like a stone at the sure knowledge that she wouldn't get an answer.

Her gaze drifted to the stairway that led up to the loft where the bedrooms were tucked, then cut to the telephone that had been ripped from the kitchen wall and now hung by slender tendons of wire.

Her heart beat faster. A fine mist of sweat slicked her palms.

"Lucy?"

"She's dead."

The words were like a pair of shotgun blasts in the still of the room. Mari wheeled around, a scream wedged in her throat right behind her heart. He stood at the other end of the table, six feet of hewn granite in faded jeans and a chambray work shirt. How anything that big could have sneaked up on her was beyond reasoning. Her perceptions distorted by fear, she thought his shoulders rivaled the mountains for size. He stood there, staring at her from beneath the low-riding brim of a dusty black Stetson, his gaze narrow, measuring, his mouth set in a grim, compressed line. His right hand—big with blunt-tipped fingers—hung at his side just inches from a holstered revolver that looked big enough to bring down a buffalo.

WARRIOR BRIDE
by
Tamara Leigh

After four years of planning revenge on the highwayman who'd stolen her future, Lizanne Balmaine had the blackguard at the point of her sword. Yet something about the onyx-eyed man she'd abducted and taken to her family estate was different—something that made her hesitate at her moment of triumph. Now she was his prisoner . . . and even more than her handsome captor she feared her own treacherous desires.

"Welcome, my Lord Ranulf," she said. "'Tis a fine day for a duel."

He stared unblinkingly at her, then let a frown settle between his eyes. "Forsooth, I did not expect you to attend this bloodletting," he said. "I must needs remember you are not a lady."

Her jaw hardened. "I assure you I would not miss this for anything," she tossed back.

He looked at the weapons she carried. "And where is this man who would champion your ill-fated cause?" he asked, looking past her.

"Man?" She shook her head. "There is no man."

Ranulf considered this, one eyebrow arched. "You were unable to find a single man willing to die for you, my lady? Not one?"

Refusing to rise to the bait, Lizanne leaned forward, smiling faintly. "Alas, I fear I am so uncomely that none would offer."

"And what of our bargain?" Ranulf asked, suspicion cast upon his voice.

"It stands."

"You think to hold me till your brother returns?" He shifted more of his weight onto his uninjured leg. "Do you forget that I am an unwilling captive, my lady? 'Tis not likely you will return me to that foul-smelling cell." He took a step toward her.

At his sudden movement, the mare shied away, snorting loudly as it pranced sideways. Lizanne brought the animal under control with an imperceptible tightening of her legs.

"Nay," she said, her eyes never wavering. "Your opponent is here before you now."

Ranulf took some moments to digest this, then burst out laughing. As preposterous as it was, a mere woman challenging an accomplished knight to a duel of swords, her proposal truly did not surprise him, though it certainly amused him.

And she was not jesting! he acknowledged. Amazingly, it fit the conclusions he had wrestled with, and finally accepted, regarding her character.

Had she a death wish, then? Even if that spineless brother of hers had shown her how to swing a sword, it was inconceivable she could have any proficiency with such a heavy, awkward weapon. A sling, perhaps, and he mustn't forget a dagger, but a sword?

Slowly, he sobered, blinking back tears of mirth and drawing deep, ragged breaths of air.

She edged her horse nearer, her indignation evident in her stiffly erect bearing. "I find no humor in the situation. Mayhap you would care to enlighten me, Lord Ranulf?"

"Doubtless, you would not appreciate my explanation, my lady."

Her chin went up. "Think you I will not make a worthy opponent?"

"With your nasty tongue, perhaps, but—"

"Then let us not prolong the suspense any longer," she snapped. Swiftly, she removed the sword from its scabbard and tossed it, hilt first, to him.

Reflexively, Ranulf pulled it from the air, his hand closing around the cool metal hilt. He was taken aback as he held it aloft, for inasmuch as the weapon appeared perfectly honed on both its edges, it was not the weighty sword he was accustomed to. Indeed, it felt awkward in his grasp.

"And what is this, a child's toy?" he quipped, twisting the sword in his hand.

In one fluid motion, Lizanne dismounted and turned to face him. "'Tis the instrument of your death, my lord." Advancing, she drew her own sword, identical to the one he held.

He lowered his sword's point and narrowed his eyes. "Think you I would fight a woman?"

"'Tis as we agreed."

"I agreed to fight a man—"

"Nay, you agreed to fight the opponent of my choice. I stand before you now ready to fulfill our bargain."

"We have no such bargain," he insisted.

"Would you break your vow? Are you so dishonorable?"

Never before had Ranulf's honor been questioned. For King Henry and, when necessary, himself, he had fought hard and well, and he carried numerous battle scars to attest to his valor. Still, her insult rankled him.

"'Tis honor that compels me to decline," he

said, a decidedly dangerous smile playing about his lips.

"Honor?" She laughed, coming to an abrupt halt a few feet from him. "Methinks 'tis your injury, coward. Surely, you can still wield a sword?"

Coward? A muscle in his jaw jerked. This one was expert at stirring the remote depths of his anger. "Were you a man, you would be dead now."

"Then imagine me a man," she retorted, lifting her sword in challenge.

The very notion was laughable. Even garbed as she was, the Lady Lizanne was wholly a woman.

"Nay, I fear I must decline." Resolutely, he leaned on the sword. "'Twill make a fine walking stick, though," he added, flexing the steel blade beneath his weight.

Ignoring his quip, Lizanne took a step nearer. "You cannot decline!"

"Aye, and I do."

"Then I will gut you like a pig!" she shouted and leaped forward.

REBEL IN SILK
by
Sandra Chastain

*"Sandra Chastain's characters' steamy relationships
are the stuff dreams are made of."
—Romantic Times*

*Dallas Burke had come to Willow Creek, Wyoming,
to find her brother's killer, and she had no intention of being scared off—not by the roughnecks who
trashed her newspaper office, nor by the devilishly
handsome cowboy who warned her of the violence to
come. Yet she couldn't deny that the tall, sunbronzed
rancher had given her something to think about,
namely, what it would be like to be held in his
steel-muscled arms and feel his sensuous mouth on
hers . . . .*

A bunch of liquored-up cowboys were riding past
the station, shooting guns into the air, bearing down
on the startled Miss Banning caught by drifts in the
middle of the street.

From the general store, opposite where Dallas
was standing, came a figure who grabbed her valise
in one hand and scooped her up with the other, flung her over his shoulder, and stepped onto
the wooden sidewalk beneath the roof over the
entrance to the saloon.

Dallas let out a shocked cry as the horses
thundered by. She might have been run over had
it not been for the man's quick action. Now,
hanging upside down, she felt her rescuer's hand

cradling her thigh in much too familiar a manner.

"Sir, what are you doing?"

"Saving your life."

The man lifted her higher, then, as she started to slide, gave her bottom another tight squeeze. Being rescued was one thing, but this was out of line. Gratitude flew out of her mind as he groped her backside.

"Put me down, you . . . you . . . lecher!"

"Gladly!" He leaned forward, loosened his grip and let her slide to the sidewalk where she landed in a puddle of melted snow and ice. The valise followed with a thump.

"Well, you didn't have to try to break my leg!" Dallas scrambled to her feet, her embarrassment tempering her fear and turning it into anger.

"No, I could have let the horses do it!"

Dallas had never heard such cold dispassion in a voice. He wasn't flirting with her. He wasn't concerned about her injuries. She didn't know why he'd bothered to touch her so intimately. One minute he was there, and the next he had turned to walk away.

"Wait, please wait! I'm sorry to appear ungrateful. I was just startled."

As she scurried along behind him, all she could see was the hat covering his face and head, his heavy canvas duster, and boots with silver spurs set with turquoise. He wasn't stopping.

Dallas reached out and caught his arm. "Now, just a minute. Where I come from, a man at least gives a lady the chance to say a proper thank you. What kind of man are you?"

"I'm cold, I'm thirsty, and I'm ready for a woman. Are you volunteering?"

There was a snickering sound that ran through the room they'd entered. Dallas raised her head and glanced around. She wasn't the only woman in the saloon, but she was the only one wearing all her clothes.

Any other woman might have gasped. But Dallas suppressed her surprise. She didn't know the layout of the town yet, and until she did, she wouldn't take a chance of offending anyone, even these ladies of pleasure. "I'm afraid not. I'm a newspaperwoman, not a . . . an entertainer."

He ripped his hat away, shaking off the glistening beads of melting snow that hung in the jet-black hair that touched his shoulders. He was frowning at her, his brow drawn into deep lines of displeasure; his lips, barely visible beneath a bushy mustache, pressed into a thin line.

His eyes, dark and deep, held her. She sensed danger and a hot intensity.

Where the man she'd met on the train seemed polished and well-mannered, her present adversary was anything but a gentleman. He was a man of steel who challenged with every glance. She shivered in response.

"Hello," a woman's voice intruded. "I'm Miranda. You must have come in on the train."

Dallas blinked, breaking the contact between her and her rescuer. With an effort, she turned to the woman.

"Ah, yes. I did. Dallas Banning." She started to hold out her hand, realized that she was clutching her valise, then lowered it. "I'm afraid I've made rather a mess of introducing myself to Green Willow Creek."

"Well, I don't know about what happened in the street, but following Jake in here might give your reputation a bit of a tarnish."

"Jake?" This was the Jake that her brother Jamie had been worried about.

"Why, yes," Miranda said, "I assumed you two knew each other?"

"Not likely," Jake growled and turned to the bar. "She's too skinny and her mouth is too big for my taste."

"Miss Banning?" Elliott Parnell, the gentleman she'd met on the train, rushed in from the street. "I saw what happened. Are you all right?"

Jake looked up, catching Dallas between him and the furious look he cast at Elliott Parnell.

Dallas didn't respond. The moment Jake had spotted Mr. Elliott, everything in the saloon had seemed to stop. All movement. All sound. For a long endless moment it seemed as if everyone in the room were frozen in place.

Jake finally spoke. "If she's with you and your sodbusters, Elliott, you'd better get her out of here."

Elliot took Dallas's arm protectively. "No, Jake. We simply came in on the same train. Miss Banning is James Banning's sister."

"Oh? The troublemaking newspaper editor. Almost as bad as the German immigrants. I've got no use for either one. Take my advice, Miss Banning. Get on the next train back to wherever you came from."

"I don't need your advice, Mr. Silver."

"Suit yourself, but somebody didn't want your brother here, and my guess is that you won't be any more welcome!"

Dallas felt a shiver of pure anger ripple down her backbone. She might as well make her position known right now. She came to find out the truth and she wouldn't be threatened. "Mr. Silver—"

"Jake! Elliott!" Miranda interrupted, a warning in her voice. "Can't you see that Miss Banning is half-frozen? Men! You have to forgive them," she said, turning to Dallas. "At the risk of further staining your reputation, I'd be pleased to have you make use of my room to freshen up and get dry. That is if you don't mind being . . . here."

"I'd be most appreciative, Miss Miranda," Dallas said, following her golden-haired hostess to the stairs.

Dallas felt all the eyes in the room boring holes in her back. She didn't have to be told where she was and what was taking place beyond the doors on either side of the corridor. If being here ruined her reputation, so be it. She wasn't here to make friends anyway. Besides, a lead to Jamie's murderer was a lot more likely to come from these people than those who might be shocked by her actions.

For just a second she wondered what would have happened if Jake had marched straight up the stairs with her. Then she shook off the impossible picture that thought had created.

She wasn't here to be bedded.

She was here to kill a man.

She just had to find out which one.

And don't miss these spectacular
romances from Bantam Books,
on sale in April:

DECEPTION
by the New York Times bestselling author
Amanda Quick
"One of the hottest and most
prolific writers in romance today . . ."
—*USA Today*

RELENTLESS
by the highly acclaimed author
Patricia Potter
"One of the romance genre's
finest talents . . ."
—*Romantic Times*

SEIZED BY LOVE
by the mistress of erotic historical romance
Susan Johnson
"Susan Johnson is one of the best."
—*Romantic Times*

WILD CHILD
by the bestselling author
Suzanne Forster
"(Suzanne Forster) is guaranteed to steam up
your reading glasses."
—*L.A. Daily News*

OFFICIAL RULES

To enter the sweepstakes below carefully follow all instructions found elsewhere in this offer.

The **Winners Classic** will award prizes with the following approximate maximum values: 1 Grand Prize: $26,500 (or $25,000 cash alternate); 1 First Prize: $3,000; 5 Second Prizes: $400 each; 35 Third Prizes: $100 each; 1,000 Fourth Prizes: $7.50 each. Total maximum retail value of Winners Classic Sweepstakes is $42,500. Some presentations of this sweepstakes may contain individual entry numbers corresponding to one or more of the aforementioned prize levels. To determine the Winners, individual entry numbers will first be compared with the winning numbers preselected by computer. For winning numbers not returned, prizes will be awarded in random drawings from among all eligible entries received. Prize choices may be offered at various levels. If a winner chooses an automobile prize, all license and registration fees, taxes, destination charges and, other expenses not offered herein are the responsibility of the winner. If a winner chooses a trip, travel must be complete within one year from the time the prize is awarded. Minors must be accompanied by an adult. Travel companion(s) must also sign release of liability. Trips are subject to space and departure availability. Certain black-out dates may apply.

The following applies to the sweepstakes named above:

No purchase necessary. You can also enter the sweepstakes by sending your name and address to: P.O. Box 508, Gibbstown, N.J. 08027. Mail each entry separately. Sweepstakes begins 6/1/93. Entries must be received by 12/30/94. Not responsible for lost, late, damaged, misdirected, illegible or postage due mail. Mechanically reproduced entries are not eligible. All entries become property of the sponsor and will not be returned.

Prize Selection/Validations: Selection of winners will be conducted no later than 5:00 PM on January 28, 1995, by an independent judging organization whose decisions are final. Random drawings will be held at 1211 Avenue of the Americas, New York, N.Y. 10036. Entrants need not be present to win. Odds of winning are determined by total number of entries received. Circulation of this sweepstakes is estimated not to exceed 200 million. All prizes are guaranteed to be awarded and delivered to winners. Winners will be notified by mail and may be required to complete an affidavit of eligibility and release of liability which must be returned within 14 days of date on notification or alternate winners will be selected in a random drawing. Any prize notification letter or any prize returned to a participating sponsor, Bantam Doubleday Dell Publishing Group, Inc., its participating divisions or subsidiaries, or the independent judging organization as undeliverable will be awarded to an alternate winner. Prizes are not transferable. No substitution for prizes except as offered or as may be necessary due to unavailability, in which case a prize of equal or greater value will be awarded. Prizes will be awarded approximately 90 days after the drawing. All taxes are the sole responsibility of the winners. Entry constitutes permission (except where prohibited by law) to use winners' names, hometowns, and likenesses for publicity purposes without further or other compensation. Prizes won by minors will be awarded in the name of parent or legal guardian.

Participation: Sweepstakes open to residents of the United States and Canada, except for the province of Quebec. Sweepstakes sponsored by Bantam Doubleday Dell Publishing Group, Inc., (BDD), 1540 Broadway, New York, NY 10036. Versions of this sweepstakes with different graphics and prize choices will be offered in conjunction with various solicitations or promotions by different subsidiaries and divisions of BDD. Where applicable, winners will have their choice of any prize offered at level won. Employees of BDD, its divisions, subsidiaries, advertising agencies, independent judging organization, and their immediate family members are not eligible.

Canadian residents, in order to win, must first correctly answer a time limited arithmetical skill testing question. Void in Puerto Rico, Quebec and wherever prohibited or restricted by law. Subject to all federal, state, local and provincial laws and regulations. For a list of major prize winners (available after 1/29/95): send a self-addressed, stamped envelope entirely separate from your entry to: Sweepstakes Winners, P.O. Box 517, Gibbstown, NJ 08027. Requests must be received by 12/30/94. DO NOT SEND ANY OTHER CORRESPONDENCE TO THIS P.O. BOX.

Don't miss these fabulous Bantam women's fiction titles

on sale in April

DECEPTION
Now available in paperback by *New York Times* bestselling author Amanda Quick
"One of the hottest and most prolific writers in romance today."—*USA Today*
❏ 56506-0 $5.99/7.50 in Canada

RELENTLESS
by Patricia Potter
Bestselling author of *Notorious*
"The healing power of love and the beauty of trust...shine like a beacon in all of Ms. Potter's work."—*Romantic Times*
❏ 56226-6 $5.50/6.99 in Canada

SEIZED BY LOVE
by the incomparable Susan Johnson
"SEIZED BY LOVE withstands the test of time... a wonderful tale."—*Affaire de Coeur*
❏ 56836-1 $5.50/6.99 in Canada

WILD CHILD
A classic romance
by the highly acclaimed Suzanne Forster
"(Suzanne Forster) is guaranteed to steam up your reading glasses."—*L.A. Daily News*
❏ 56837-X $4,50/5.99 in Canada

Ask for these books at your local bookstore or use this page to order.

❏ Please send me the books I have checked above. I am enclosing $ _____ (add $2.50 to cover postage and handling). Send check or money order, no cash or C. O. D.'s please.

Name _____

Address _____

City/ State/ Zip _____

Send order to: Bantam Books, Dept. FN137, 2451 S. Wolf Rd., Des Plaines, IL 60018
Allow four to six weeks for delivery.
Prices and availability subject to change without notice.   FN137 4/94

The Very Best in Contemporary Women's Fiction

Sandra Brown

_____	28951-9 TEXAS! LUCKY	$5.99/6.99 in Canada
_____	28990-X TEXAS! CHASE	$5.99/6.99
_____	29500-4 TEXAS! SAGE	$5.99/6.99
_____	29085-1 22 INDIGO PLACE	$5.99/6.99
_____	29783-X A WHOLE NEW LIGHT	$5.99/6.99
_____	56045-X TEMPERATURES RISING	$5.99/6.99
_____	56274-6 FANTA C	$4.99/5.99
_____	56278-9 LONG TIME COMING	$4.99/5.99

Tami Hoag

_____	29534-9 LUCKY'S LADY	$4.99/5.99
_____	29053-3 MAGIC	$4.99/5.99
_____	56050-6 SARAH'S SIN	$4.50/5.50
_____	29272-2 STILL WATERS	$4.99/5.99
_____	56160-X CRY WOLF	$5.50/6.50
_____	56161-8 DARK PARADISE	$5.99/7.50

Nora Roberts

_____	29078-9 GENUINE LIES	$5.99/6.99
_____	28578-5 PUBLIC SECRETS	$5.99/6.99
_____	26461-3 HOT ICE	$5.99/6.99
_____	26574-1 SACRED SINS	$5.99/6.99
_____	27859-2 SWEET REVENGE	$5.99/6.99
_____	27283-7 BRAZEN VIRTUE	$5.99/6.99
_____	29597-7 CARNAL INNOCENCE	$5.50/6.50
_____	29490-3 DIVINE EVIL	$5.99/6.99

Deborah Smith

_____	29107-6 MIRACLE	$4.50/5.50
_____	29092-4 FOLLOW THE SUN	$4.99/5.99
_____	28759-1 THE BELOVED WOMAN	$4.50/5.50
_____	29690-6 BLUE WILLOW	$5.50/6.50
_____	29689-2 SILK AND STONE	$5.99/6.99

Theresa Weir

_____	56092-1 LAST SUMMER	$4.99/5.99
_____	56378-5 ONE FINE DAY	$4.99/5.99

Ask for these titles at your bookstore or use this page to order.

Please send me the books I have checked above. I am enclosing $ _____ (add $2.50 to cover postage and handling). Send check or money order, no cash or C. O. D.'s please.

Mr./ Ms. _____

Address _____

City/ State/ Zip _____

Send order to: Bantam Books, Dept. FN 24, 2451 S. Wolf Road, Des Plaines, IL 60018

Please allow four to six weeks for delivery.

Prices and availability subject to change without notice.

FN 24 4/94